A.B. FINLAYSON

Rock Zombie

One Night in Redcar with the Dead

First edition

Cover art by Laura @Hello_Moon_Creative

This book was professionally typeset on Reedsy.
Find out more at reedsy.com

Contents

Author's Note

This novel is set in a real town… my hometown of Redcar on the northeast coast of England. All of the pubs, clubs, parks, squares, streets, shops and side-alleys described are very real places and many still exist today (or they did in the '90s when this story is set). In fact, you could quite easily walk the route the characters take and stop in for a drink, a dance, a play, or something to eat along the way (if you do, please take photos and tag me in them, that would be excellent!)

Despite the real locations, the characters are all entirely fictitious. Every teenager, barman, waitress, copper, soldier, drinker, dancer, raver, bell-ringer, priest, butcher, baker, candlestick maker, zombie, and ghost is a product of my overactive imagination. Any resemblance to real people, living or dead, is purely coincidental.

This silly story is a bit of a love letter to the '90s and, as such, it contains references to many TV shows, movies, characters, bands, and songs from the era. Every chapter is the title of a song, but no lyrics or quotes are reproduced anywhere in this novel, except for those that are in the public domain.

Dedication

To Louise

Whose 'fact checking' for Rock Zombie told me far more about my big sister than I really wanted to know.

Cigarettes & Alcohol

We are obsessed with death because it is one of the few things we know nothing about. Forget what the religions say, they're guessing. No one has come back and said, "Hey, you know what, it's not so bad up there. The music is shit and there aren't enough chairs, but the finger food is alright."

Whichever way you look at it, death is a bugger. We're obsessed with it, consumed by it, driven by it... because we're scared of the things we don't understand. Highway to Hell or Stairway to Heaven? But no one has a map.

Little wonder then that teenagers in the '90s hung out in graveyards and parks, sitting in circles, passing around cigarettes and bottles of illegally procured booze—it wasn't just because there was sod all to do and some handy seats. It was because their brains were waking up to the inevitability of the human condition and how terrifyingly fragile we really are.

We're born. We live. We die. From the cradle to the grave with a cheeky finger or hand-shandy behind the mausoleum on a weekend. Anything to finally find something worth living for.

This story takes place in the northeast town of Redcar, but it could be any British seaside, really. Quiet, unassuming, a relatively peaceful place of chip shops, pleasant parks, and more pound shops than you can shake a stick of rock at. But there's always something bubbling beneath the surface, some drama waiting to unfold to put that small town firmly on the map. If years of British soaps have taught us anything, it's that small towns breed big problems. For this one night in Redcar, it's apocalyptic. But we'll get to that.

In the beach park, where we lay our scene, we have a haven for mums and dads with young kids, complete with a paddling pool and the obligatory hard metal see-saw, swing set, and roundabout that marks every British play park.[1] When the sun is up, the Stray—as it is known—is lovely and peaceful, a riot of colour: bright green grass, golden sand, and the bloody freezing blue waters of the North Sea. The big red-brick houses lining the Coast Road have the luxury of ocean views, which is nice if you like that sort of thing, but most of the time it's pissing down, and you can barely see the convoy of colourful container ships sitting on the horizon beneath heavy black clouds.

When the sun goes down, however, that's when the Stray comes to life (which is ironic, considering where this is going). The families and dog-walkers are replaced by tracksuit-clad scallies, and boot-cut Indie kids in their flannels or army jackets. Back then, it seemed like two different worlds, but the differences were simple. Tracksuits or jeans. White Lightning or lager. Happy hardcore, pill-popping, whistle-posses, or guitar-wielding, black nail polish-sporting poets. But no matter how you're dressed, who you are, or which side of the tracks you come from, everyone was doing the same thing; getting shit-faced for cheap before trying to get into one of the many pubs and clubs in town. And if that didn't work then it's back to the parks and graveyards for a late-night fumble in the dark.

It didn't matter what clothes you wore because we're all just skin sacks of meat and gristle underneath, but it *is* easier to wank someone off in a pair of trackies than through some Levis.

---

[1] It wasn't just the laissez-faire approach to children's safety that left generations of British kids with painful scars and brands, their own stupidity resulted in a fair number of impromptu *rites de passage*. Every week some teenage girl would squeeze into the kids' swing and get herself stuck, but it didn't matter. This was long before everyone had a camera phone in their pocket, so they were free to make twats of themselves without it being shared with the world. Halcyon days.

Self Esteem

Rob held the wrap in nervous fingers. It was small. Just a tightly folded piece of paper ripped from the corner of a *Melody Maker* magazine. Hard to see what all the fuss was about really, but it had been given to him by Vikki, and Vikki was, well... *Vikki.*

Every group had a Vikki. The popular. The unassailably attractive. The terrifyingly experienced. And then there's Rob. Who wasn't.

Until recently.

It's amazing how quickly things can change, sometimes it only takes one night. Like last Saturday, for example, when Rob went on *Stars in Their Eyes.*

"Tonight, Matthew. I'm going to be... Kurt Cobain!"

Prime-time television. Dressed like, looking like, and sounding like a grunge icon. It was a far cry from the quiet kid no one paid attention to in the beehive of matching blazers and ties. Yes, life had changed, and suddenly all the old rules and regulations of high school hierarchy no longer applied.

Come as you are.

So, he did. Ripped jeans, black t-shirt, and knackered Converse—the *Wayne's World* uniform.

Normally, Rob would be at home with his parents at this time on a Saturday night, flicking between *Catchphrase, Casualty,* and whatever movie was on before *The Jerry Springer Show,* but Vikki had text and now she had a look in her eye. He knew that look. He'd seen that look—on *Hollyoaks,* mainly, but he'd seen it. Suddenly, all the words he'd practised on the way to the park vanished as he lost his nerve.

"Sorted for Es and Wizz?" Wayne asked in a perfectly timed moment of distraction. The ginger drug dealer appeared between them with a wide grin and the world's longest cigarette dangling from his mouth. It wasn't a joint. It was a Berkley Red. His dad got them duty-free on the bottle run to Amsterdam. "More space to squeeze in some speed," he reckoned. Wayne had gone from dealing in the playground to dealing in the parks and pubs without so much as a pause for breath. He always had tweezers and a pocket full of carefully folded wraps. He was the origami king of the beach park, dancing through the tracksuit-clad masses as they fumbled in the dark while the air filled with sweet, tangy smoke and the scent of regret. Wayne patted them both on the shoulder and grinned again. "Let me know what you think of the new gear," he said with a wink, then wandered off on his rounds.

To be clear, Rob is seventeen. They all are. Out of school but hanging onto the familiar for dear life. Not quite ready to take the plunge into adulthood, but equally desperate for something more. For the local kids, the beach park acted as a median strip between two worlds, a way to ease from one life to another. You need water for baptism after all, though a pissy kids' pool probably isn't the most sanitary of fonts. For Rob, this was all new, terrifyingly new, and he clung to the wrap with sweaty fingers.

"Are you going to take that?" Vikki asked.

"I'll save it for later," he said, finally, stuffing it in his pocket and taking a long drink from a can of lager he'd bought on the way here. Rob hadn't been checked for ID in over a year, but that still didn't settle the nerves whenever he ducked into The Wine Lodge. He was no stranger to booze, he'd been raised on Babycham at Christmas and shandies with Sunday dinner, and he'd spent a fair number of Saturday nights since leaving school sharing cans with his dad, but drugs were something else. He sighed. Was that really the difference between adulthood and being a kid? You go from form class in school to class As in the park? It seemed like a particularly disappointing cliché, but here he was. Out and about. Sitting on a wall within touching distance of Vikki, who, for whatever reason, had suddenly taken a shine to him. It was a total mystery. Surely nothing to do with the fact he was the only kid from school who had been on TV without a mugshot.

It should be made clear here that Rob may be a bit dumb, but he's not a dick. This was *the* Vikki Abraham we're talking about. If they did yearbooks back then her entry might have been something along the lines of,

'Vikki Abraham - Fittest Lass.'

Rob, on the other hand, drifted through school while things happened to other people.

'Robert Neville - Was Also There.'

It was different now, though; people knew who he was. He'd been on TV. He was front page of *The Evening Gazette*. He was going on *TFM Radio* in two days and *The Big Breakfast* next week, but none of that mattered, because *the* Vikki Abraham had invited him to the park to hang with the cool kids.

Rob took a drink and tried to act cool, whatever that meant.

"I could've picked you up if I'd known you were definitely going to come," Vikki said. He glanced at her and then looked away. She had blue eyes. The kind that hypnotise young men. He took another drink, a long one, and tried to think of something to say.

"You drove?" he managed after some painful contemplation. It wasn't dazzling but it was a start. Vikki smiled. Oh God. He was in trouble.

"Yeah, Dad got me a car for my birthday. He's the best. I parked up the Stray. You know that little car park on Coast Road?"

"The one where…"

"The one where you nearly broke your neck that year. That's right," she laughed. Rob had been going to say the one where people go to shag in the backseat, but Vikki had steered the conversation down memory lane, and he didn't dare bring it back. "You were showing off," she said, nudging him and not moving away. Her body rested against his. He could smell her hair.

"Pretty girls and Mad Dog 20/20," Rob said in a flash of daring. "Makes little boys do daft things." There was a moment of silence while his face burned, and he took a swig of lager.

"You think I'm pretty?" Vikki asked and the tone of her voice had shifted. It was unmistakable, even for Rob. There was far more in those few words than a simple question and they both knew it. Rob finished the can.

"Of course. You're the prettiest girl I know."

He looked at her and she looked back. Eyes flicked to lips and returned. Vikki leaned in.

And someone screamed.

In the middle of the park, a girl in the world's shortest black skirt and oversized Diesel puffer jacket had her arms in the air and was beating at a boy who staggered against a picnic table, laughing as he tried to protect his face. A horde of girlfriends extricated themselves from various clutches and swarmed over.

"What's going on, Kaz?"

"This nobhead!" the girl said, slapping the laughing boy again. "He tried to finger me with gloves on!"

"It's fucking cold!" he laughed, ducking another hit.

"Jesus Christ!" Rob said with a shake of his head.

"What?"

"Well, it's just like the playground, isn't it? Nothing changes."

"Some things change."

"Like what?"

"Well, I've got a car. You wanna see?"

And there it was—the unspoken words between the spoken ones. Rob was a mad cow staring down both barrels of the farmer's gun, about to fumble some ill-conceived excuse, but Vikki pulled him from the wall before he could say a word.

* * *

Wayne Dickson swore under his breath. He'd told Vikki to try the new stuff in the park, but she always got horny after a few lines. He'd just have to wait until they were finished. By the look on Rob's face, it wouldn't take long.

Sex & Candy

Vikki took off her bra and Rob came in his jeans, mortified as he gasped and hunched over, pleasure and pain rippling through him. He would've run right then and there if Vikki hadn't pressed her body to his and stuck her tongue in his mouth. *Oh God, she hasn't noticed. An own goal before the match has even started! And what is that?*! Vikki put something in his mouth. It dissolved slowly like the sugar papers on a Gregg's cupcake. Rob swallowed and his mind exploded. He gasped again. Vikki sat up as she fumbled at his jeans. She shivered and her skin prickled with goosebumps. Rob looked at her breasts. He giggled. He had never seen boobs before. Well, not in the flesh so to speak, though there were plenty of Wonder Bra adverts in the mail-order catalogues at home. This, though, was the live show. Vikki's boobs glowed in the orange light washing through the rear window of her car. Rob was hypnotised. The fine, minuscule hairs raised on firm flesh fascinated him, and there was the flicker of a pulse beneath the curved skin. Vikki grabbed the forgotten wrap from Rob's unresisting fingers and opened the origami treasure trove like one of those chatterbox fortune tellers the girls made in school. *Pick a number, pick a colour, pick a number.* But this was no game. She poured powder into a cigarette paper and folded it with shaking fingers.

"All yours," she said.

Rob didn't move. He couldn't. He stared at Vikki as she grinned at him, her eyes wild and unfocused. She sat forward and thrust the wrap towards his mouth, laughing at how scared and frozen he was. Then she kissed him again. Long and hard and passionate, like she'd seen in the movies.

Never mind *Stars in Their Eyes. This* was the single greatest moment of Rob's life!

It was also the last.

Good Riddance (Time of Your Life)

Rob blinked as the orange streetlight washed the backseat of the car in a golden tableau. Vikki was dead. There was none of that, "it took him a moment to realise what he was looking at" nonsense; he knew it instantly. Vikki was dead. Very dead. Her body was bent backwards, almost folded in two, her head hanging to the side and her eyes staring, but it was the gaping wound in her throat that really gave the game away. White bone shone through the red mess, while flaps of skin lay in ragged folds. Her mouth was open, her lips and teeth stained with blood. The dangly thing no one knows the name of sat like a frightened worm in the recess, and because some clichés are worthy of use, there was blood everywhere. It covered the backseat of the car and Vikki's arched body like paint. A gruesome, northern *Goldfinger* but Roger Moore was nowhere in sight. The door next to her was open, and Vikki's arm hung limp in the night. Rob took it all in as he staggered back, falling out of the car with a cry of horror.

He got to his feet and stood trembling in the car park. The world was different. He noticed the strangeness of it immediately—which was remarkable considering he barely noticed he had just fallen through a closed door. Rob rubbed his eyes, trying to clear away the horrors, but it was no use. An image sat emblazoned on his soul, rising above the blood, the lifeless eyes, and reaching hand. It was a photograph, a still frame in his mind, a clear picture of a large bite on Vikki's left tit.

An actual bite. A human one. A cartoon chunk from an apple. Complete with regulation teeth marks.

Rob turned towards town and then back. There were no headlights on the road, no cars for him to flag down, no people out for a stroll. The mist had rolled in in that way it often does at this time of year, a slow but steady wall of white suffusing lights into wide auras. An unnecessary accoutrement, Rob felt. He fumbled in his pockets for his phone, but his searching fingers came up empty.

It must be in the car.

Rob stared at the silver vehicle again: the windows fogged up like *that* scene in Titanic; the bodywork glistening with the moisture brought by the mist. It was so normal, except for the door, yawning open in a portentous reminder of the horrors within.

Rob rubbed his hands over his face, but he couldn't feel a thing. *Must be shock*, he thought, and then something moved.

There was a dark figure on the very edge of the cloying mists. An old man, his back bent and head down. Rob called out, then strangled it. Maybe it wasn't such a good idea to draw attention to himself with a murderous bloody nutter on the loose?

But then… things were different.

Rob looked at the car, then looked at the patch of mist that swirled and filled in the space where the man had been. He knew he shouldn't leave the scene; he knew he shouldn't follow someone who might well be a psycho killer—that this was the start of every clichéd horror movie there was—but he also knew with a strange certainty that he wasn't afraid. Not even a little bit. It was intoxicating.

His mind made up; he strode after the vanishing figure.

Otherside

In some deep recess of whatever passes for a soul, Rob probably knew he was dead the moment his "eyes" opened, and he saw Vikki, but some habits are hard to break. New realities can take a bit to settle in—like when PJ and Duncan started calling themselves Ant and Dec, or Marathon Bars changed their name to Snickers. Thankfully, Rob was a lot faster than those glacial, cultural shifts and though he was going slow, he was getting there. By the time he reached the other side of the car park, he'd have it.

It was the lack of fear that did it.

Sure, he had fallen back in shock, but shock is largely in the mind. Fear is more the preserve of chemicals and a central nervous system. Now he no longer had those things, his mind was free to make deductions quicker than Miss Marple.

"Hey!" he called. No fear. No anxiety. No hesitation. What a rush! "Oy! I'm talking to you."

The mists thinned and the shambling old man came back into view. He walked with a limp, shuffling and scraping his feet across the gravel.

"Hey! Stop!"

He didn't stop.

He didn't pay any attention to Rob. He just kept going. Rob reached out and put his hand on the man's shoulder.

Then he tried again.

On the third attempt, he let out a nervous laugh and looked at his fingers. He wiggled them and the penny dropped.

Sixth Sense style.

Rob walked around the shuffling figure, suspecting he could've walked through him, but that didn't seem right. He looked at his face and blinked. It wasn't an old man at all. He was quite young in fact. Say, oh, about seventeen.

Rob laughed. What else could he do?

"Fuck," he said, rooted to the spot as the figure kept coming.

It was him.

The shuffling man was Rob.

High and Dry

Rob followed his body in a daze. Blood covered the lower half of the face and there were little dags of flesh between the teeth. Some spiritual part of him wanted to vomit but he just stared at the creature that was him and yet not him. The eyes were hard, like steel. The thing let out a moan as it moved.

"I'm a fucking zombie!" Rob said in a quiet voice, and then his body walked through him. He shivered despite no longer having the necessary equipment and looked down. "*And* a ghost! Well... fuck!" he said. "Fucking fuck!" Because some words can do all the heavy lifting.

Rob's zombie walked into a high tide sign and grunted. Rob laughed. The whole situation was so ridiculous it felt like a *Fast Show* sketch, and he stood there, momentarily staring into the strangest funhouse mirror as he tried to make sense of things. The body moved, stepping under the glow of the last streetlight, and Rob saw himself without the baggage or judgements we all needlessly level at ourselves. He looked older, somehow. Handsome. The lines were hard, the jaw more solid and pronounced. *You know what?* he thought for the first time in his... life, *I'm actually quite fit.*

Rob was still admiring himself when his body walked through him and tumbled off the edge of a dune. It rag-dolled onto the beach, landed face-down in the sand, and farted.

* * *

The mist hung heavy now, clinging to the silver body of the Vauxhall Cavalier. The whole world was suffused with fog, the lights of the distant houses dull, faded glows, and the town itself nowhere to be seen, swallowed by the weather. A car crept along the road, headlights like fireflies. It turned towards the car park and trundled over the gravel; the soft crunching tyres the only sound. Light washed over the silent Vauxhall and the driver turned off the engine, the warm metal ticking as it cooled in the evening air. A door opened and a man stepped out. He lit a cigarette, which glowed as he sucked on the end, and he looked at the open door of the other car. A hand reached into the night, the fingers bunching into a fist then stretching as a woman moaned.

"Bloody doggers," he muttered and opened the back door of his car. He whistled for Tricksy, but she didn't come. Normally the daft bugger flew out. He leaned in. The beautiful Dalmatian sat quivering in the footwell. He whistled again. "Come on, girl. What's got into you?" But the frightened animal refused to move. She stayed exactly where she was and whined. The man leaned over the seat, reaching for his dog, so he didn't see the figure crawl from the rear of the silver car behind him.

Grateful When You're Dead

The ghost of Robert Neville heard the screams dance through the fog. They didn't last long. The echoes faded until all that remained was the shift and slip of the distant tide caressing the sand, but Rob had his own problems. He was dead for a start. Although it seemed his body hadn't got the memo. He stared at himself. The blood was gone from his face, scrubbed clean by the sand, but the memory of it remained firmly fixed in his mind. That, and the bite on Vikki's breast. It had been him, hadn't it? Well… *that*.

"You killed her," he said.

His body thrashed half-heartedly, and Rob walked away, feeling nauseous, but then realised he wasn't. Not really. He stopped before the coming tide, entirely lost in the white blanket, standing on endless sand in a grey world.

"Is this it?" he said, his voice barely more than a whisper. He sank to his knees—aware even as he did that this was all a bit melodramatic. He looked behind him. There were no footprints. Rob stared at the featureless white mists and suddenly snapped, his face contorting with desperate sadness. "Where are you?!" he screamed. "Get off your fucking cloud and come get me! What is this? *Silent Hill*?!"

That game usually scared the bejeebus out of Rob, but he wasn't afraid. Not now. He was angry and almost consumed by sadness, but he wasn't scared. Clarity of thought is a wondrous thing when no longer encumbered by the attachments of the body. That was Hinduism, he was sure of it. Kula Shaker were always banging on about it in songs like *Govinda* and *Tattva*.

He loved that band. He watched them at Middlesbrough Town Hall for his birthday—his first real gig. They had that song; what was it called? *Grateful When You're Dead*.

Pricks.

He tried to remember the lyrics, the guitar riff drifting through the recesses of whatever passed for his consciousness. It was something about leaving the sad world behind and being happy in the afterlife, wasn't it?

Double pricks.

He was too young. There were things he wanted to do. He had been in the middle of the most important one when it happened.

"Wait a minute," he said, getting to his feet as a few latent dominoes tumbled into one another. He turned in the direction of the car park.

They both took the same drugs, and they both died. If *he* came back, then...

"Vikki."

Rob started to run.

The Man Who Sold the World

Wayne Dickson watched two girls dancing on the picnic tables. They'd bought a couple of pills and suddenly thought the beach park was the Hacienda. To be honest, he didn't think they could be that high on the shite he'd sold them, but they were only kids.

He sighed and rolled a joint. The night wasn't going as planned. Everyone was leaving, too cold and too wet in the sudden cloying mists. The older lot, the ones already eighteen or looking it, had made their way down town. They'd head to The Hydro, then work their way back, stopping at whatever club would let them in. Inevitably, though, everyone ended up at Kudos. It was the club closest to the taxis and the best kebabs. A night out in Redcar was pretty much a walk from one end of the high street to the other.

Wayne preferred the park, the young ones were always good for business, but his boss wanted him to push this new stuff and he hadn't seen Vikki since she left with the guitar kid. She was his most reliable tester. Always had been. The number of times they sat huddled on the playground sniffing glue at lunch before trying to get through double German off their tits. Mint. On one memorable occasion, Vikki threw up in the bin and blamed it on the baked beans and Turkey Twizzlers. The bin had been one of those wire mesh jobs. It wasn't pretty.

A piercing shriek of rusting iron broke the stillness and Wayne turned. There she was. He couldn't see her face in the mist, but he'd recognise that figure anywhere.

"Fit as fuck," he said, swallowing a small wrap of speed and walking towards his favourite customer.

* * *

There were two cars in the car park now, both with their doors open as though reaching out to shake hands. Rob ran to the Vauxhall and peered inside. It was empty. Vikki was gone. He heard a whimper and turned.

For the second time that evening, he wondered if ghosts could throw up.

A man sat huddled in the back of the other car, cuddling his knees like a child. His ear and nose were missing, ripped from his face in two jagged wounds, the rattling air coming through his ruined mouth in sharp hisses. As Rob watched, the grip on his legs gave way and the man slumped forward. He fell, face-first into the footwell, frightening a quivering Dalmatian.

"It's okay, girl," Rob said automatically, not thinking, but the dog's ears turned towards him like satellites. Rob gasped and stared, the implications not so much sinking in as floundering for breath on the surface, but then screams broke the stillness of the night once more and they both turned. There was no mistaking where they had come from. "The Beach Park," Rob said, and he ran again, vanishing into the mists that didn't have to part to let him through.

On the floor of the car, the dead man's fingers twitched, and the eyes snapped open. They were hard and metallic.

The Dalmatian growled.

A deep, dormant growl.

Domestic dogs are descended from wolves. Despite years of breeding and the ridiculous haircuts imposed on them by their owners, some of them have not forgotten.

Parklife

Vikki Abraham was standing half-naked in the middle of the beach park when Rob arrived. She wasn't alone. Two cowering girls in tiny skirts hugged each other on a picnic table and Wayne Dickson stood between them, utterly confused. He had seen Vikki's tits many times before, but, well, there was usually *more* of them. The fact her head drooped alarmingly to one side due to the lack of flesh in her neck really added to the overall impression that something was very fucking wrong indeed. Wayne held an object in his right hand that dangled towards the floor and his left was raised towards Vikki, warding her off. He took a swing at the dead girl as Rob ran through the fence.

"Vikki! Are you here?" Rob shouted, looking for her ghost. "It's Rob! I came back as well. Where are you? Are... are those nunchucks?!"

Wayne Dickson heard nothing and flicked the strange weapon at the dead girl.

"What are you, a fucking Ninja Turtle?"

Vikki's corpse growled and moved. Her mouth was open, her gun-metal eyes fixed on Wayne. Time slowed. Rob saw the drug dealer set his shoulders and shift his feet; he saw the curl in the upper corner of Vikki's mouth; and, ever the gentleman, he stepped between them.

Rob lifted his hands to split them apart and achieved... sod all.

But it did give him a spectacular view of the nunchuck smashing into Vikki's face after whistling through his own.

Wayne grunted as he put all his blitzed-out strength and fear into the swing.

It was a good one. Abject terror and methamphetamine will do that to a person.

Vikki's skull fractured at the temple and her left eye ruptured. Her skin split, but there was no blood. Just a strange, dark ooze. She staggered but somehow stayed upright, turning to Wayne and raising her hands. Driven on by terror and drugs, the ginger ninja charged the dead girl with an incoherent scream. Vikki snarled, her mouth opening to reveal bloodied teeth and the big lad panicked and kicked her in the chest. He stumbled back, setting his feet and flexing like a fighter in a dodgy martial arts movie.

"Prat," Rob said.

Vikki crashed violently into the roundabout, smashing her head off the metal handles but it barely slowed her down. She growled and hauled herself to her feet.

"Fuck." Rob said.

"Fuck." Wayne said.

"Fuck!" the girls screamed.

Now, there are some decisions people make while high that make no sense in the sober light of day, add to that a liberal amount of life-threatening terror and Rob guessed Wayne could be excused anything given the circumstances, but he still laughed when the red-head wannabe drug-lord dropped his nunchucks, took hold of the roundabout and began to pull.

Wayne heaved with all his might to get Vikki away from him but of course, she came right back around, reaching and growling as the well-oiled contraption spun faster and faster.

Wayne ducked.

Then kept pulling.

Then ducked again.

"Jesus wept," Rob said.

The zombie of Vikki Abraham spun through the mists, a horse short of a carousel, reaching for Wayne with each passing rotation.

"Help me!" Wayne screamed.

"I'm not going anywhere near that!" one of the girls cried. "What's wrong with her?"

"Have you... never seen... *Return of... the Living Dead?*" Wayne shouted, the exertion making his words come in rhythm with the pulls. He ducked as Vikki made a wild swing.

"There's no such thing as zombies!"

"Tell that... to her!" Wayne screamed. He was tiring now, realising he'd messed up. Tiger by the tail. Zombie on a roundabout. Either way, if he let go, he was going in a sandwich. "Please!"

Finally, one of the girls clambered slowly to the ground while her friend adopted the foetal position.

"What do I do?" she said, creeping closer, trying to keep the zombie in view. Her head moved as she watched.

"Spin!" Wayne gasped. "I'll... kill it!"

Rob was impressed. They were dealing with an undead topless woman on a kid's roundabout remarkably well. The drugs probably helped. The girl was terrified, but she stepped forward and stood behind Wayne as he reached and pulled.

"Ready?" Wayne spat and then stepped back. The girl fumbled the first two tries, and screamed as Vikki's hands lashed out, searching for something tasty. Finally, she ducked in and grabbed the bars, pulling with all her strength and nearly flying off her feet. Wayne ran for his nunchucks. The girl danced away from the snarling Vikki and jumped in to pull again, getting the rhythm of it. Pull, pull, duck. Pull, pull, duck. The zombie moved in a blur, leaning out with the centrifugal force and suddenly Wayne was back. He smashed the nunchucks into her face with a visceral scream that was less Ninja Turtle and more Scooby-Doo. He twirled the weapon, dancing on his toes as Vikki turned, hitting her again on the next pass. The thought that Wayne must have spent hours practising in front of his bedroom mirror took the varnish off the moment for Rob, but the next hit was perfect and the nunchucks wedged deep into Vikki's skull. Wayne fell to the ground, exhausted. So did the girl. Vikki's body slumped over as the roundabout slowed, and the bloody weapon dragged across the floor with a strange clack, clack, clack. Rob followed it, his head turning in small circles until eventually it stopped.

"Wheel... of... Fortune." he said to himself, but no one heard.

"Is she dead?" the girl gasped.

"Fucking hope so," Wayne said, fumbling in his pockets. "That was a lot harder than it looks in the movies." He lit one of his specially prepared Berkley Reds and sat back, taking a long draw. Half the cigarette was gone by the time he breathed out.

"What do we do now?"

"Go back to mine and get high as fuck," Wayne said. He'd had enough. The night had definitely not turned out the way he expected.

"Hadn't we better ring the police?" the girl on the table said, her voice trembling. Her eyes were wild and darted from her friend to Wayne, to the dead girl and back, passing through Rob as they did.

"Fuck that!" Wayne said, his hands shaking.

"You just beat a girl to death!"

"She was already dead!"

"How do we know?"

"The big fucking hole in her neck was my first clue!"

"I think we should go to the police," she insisted. "Lyndsey, what do you think?"

Her friend turned. Her eyes wild. "I want to get high," she said.

"Excellent," Wayne said and got to his feet. "Come on, ladies. My casa is Sue's casa." He offered a hand to Lyndsey. "But you've got to pay for the gear. I'm not a charity."

The ghost of Robert Neville watched as the biggest dickhead in school walked over to a girl he had just bludgeoned to death and pulled his nunchucks from her head. The noise was appalling, but it was the thick, wet splat after that was worse. Wayne didn't seem to notice, he put his arm around a cute girl who had just helped him accomplish a terrifying act of violence and walked out of the park as though this was just another night on the town. The other girl lingered. She cast her eyes towards the slumped body of Vikki Abraham and a shudder ran through her. Then she turned and ran after her friend.

"Now what?" Rob said to no one. He looked at Vikki, but she was entirely unhelpful.

What I Got

Rob sat on the swings and stared at the slumped body of what used to be the fittest lass in school.

None of it made sense. He was dead. He knew he was dead. Anyone walking past now would see nothing more than a child's swing drifting back and forth in the breeze (and a girl bludgeoned to death on the roundabout but that's by the by). He kicked his feet and the swing picked up momentum.

"How?"

It wasn't just his arse on the plastic or his feet on the ground, he was holding the chains! He looked at them, a series of metal links turned brown by the weather. They held the seat in place, and in turn, his backside off the floor. He tried to grip them again and his fingers passed right through. He wobbled a bit and somehow caught his balance.

"There's got to be a reason," Rob said, and then, because he'd spent his short life immersed in music, a beat filtered into his subconscious. He nodded along and hummed lyrics to himself while he tried to make sense of everything.

There are rhythms and patterns in the universe none of us can hope to comprehend, some say it is evidence of a divine creator, others say it's dumb luck or LSD, but ask any teenager who has ever looked out of a car window in the rain while the radio syncs with the rivulets and drops on the glass; they know. They know there is poetry out there. They know the universe has a soundtrack. They know this because they've all imagined being in a music video, and in Rob's moment of deep, painful introspection, the universe was about to line up with the music in his head in a weird and wonderful way.

He sang the first verse of Sublime's 'What I Got,' and when he reached a line he'd never quite understood—a line about a Dalmatian—an actual Dalmatian ran through the park. It had its head down, its ears flat, and its tail tucked tight. Rob watched it go in silence. What could he say? There was nothing particularly unusual about a dog roaming the park, but the fact it was covered in blood and carried a human hand in its mouth was a bit odd.

What's black and white and red all over?

Rob looked at Vikki and his train of thought flashed to the dead man in the car. Then he thought of his own body, floundering facedown somewhere on the beach. The thoughts stacked one on top of the other, not so much a neat pile as a derailment.

Yet again, he ran.

He was getting quite a lot of exercise for a dead guy.

Zombie

Rob found his body where he left it. Facedown, arse up. And it wasn't alone. The faceless man from the car was there.

"Don't eat me, you bastard!" Rob screamed as he dove headlong from the top of the dune. It was a decent rugby tackle, truth be told, or it would have been if he hadn't flown straight through the dead man. He rolled in panic and got to his feet as the deformed creature reached out. Rob wondered what the hell was powering him. *Night of the Living Dead* did the rounds in his street when he was a kid. Good old bootleg VHS with the tracking so bad it was like watching through snow, but it wasn't exactly a documentary. The one-armed man stumbled forward and accidentally kicked Rob's body, flipping the dead teenager onto his side as he headed towards the sea. "Hey!" Rob shouted, but he was gone, fading away like the picture on an old tube television and Rob was left with his body, which, released from its sandpit, stood up.

"You're a zombie," Rob said, feeling the inexplicable need to explain the inexplicable. The sand had managed to shift his hair into a style that looked annoyingly cool. Rob thought that was a bit unfair. He'd spent hours trying to get that *just got out of bed* scruff with his mam's giant can of mousse. Apparently, all he had to do was rub his head in the sand and shake it back and forth a bit.

Oh, and die.

"You're a zombie and I'm a ghost," Rob said, and giggled. The exertion and crazed excitement of the last hour was wearing off, and reality, such as it was, came knocking at the door of whatever now passed for his mind. "I'm dead. But I'm *there*. And I'm *here*. And apparently, there's no heaven or hell!"

Rob was alone on the beach. Well, *they* were alone. The one-armed man had vanished like Dr Richard Kimble.

"So, what the hell do I do now? I can't be the only ghost kicking around. Where are all the rest? Hello?!" he shouted into the mists, but his voice just vanished beneath the gentle roll of the coming tide. There wasn't even the comfort of an echo. Behind him, Rob's body twitched and turned towards the sea. "Oy!" he cried. "Not you as well, you doyle! How are you even doing that? You're dead!" He looked at his body and his body looked right through him with eyes like steelies.[2] "You look like a fucking model!" Rob groaned. "That's not fair. I didn't know I was that good looking. I would've done… something."

Rob's body wasn't the least bit interested in its discorporated soul's introspection and set off towards the growing rumble of the sea. Rob walked alongside, waving his hands in front of his face, but he ignored himself and kept moving.

The water was close now, he could see it bleeding forward in dark, shallow stains before rolling back. It looked calm but that didn't matter. The North Sea was the North Sea. Like a tracksuit scally on a Stella binge, it could turn violent at any moment.

The mists parted poetically, and the moon lit the ocean in a dazzling dance of silver light, picking out the glistening bald head of the one-armed man already far out in the water. White breakers tumbled and churned, and Rob watched as the man vanished. He turned to his own body with rising panic. He knew it didn't make sense, he knew it probably wouldn't make a blind bit of difference, that in fact, it might actually help matters if he didn't have to worry about his physical form wandering around eating people, but damn it, that was his body!

He screamed and shouted, flailing ethereal arms to try and push himself out of the way, to make himself change direction, but his efforts were entirely

2 Marbles. If you know, you know.

useless, his hands as insubstantial as smoke. Converse All-Stars splashed in the shallows and Rob realised he no longer had to worry about watching his body get eaten… he was going to watch it drown!

There were two things that caused the younger Robert Neville to leap into bed with his parents. One was the short-lived period of dark dreams after watching horror movies with the kids next door, the other was a series of recurring nightmares about drowning. He still had those, but at seventeen it probably wasn't appropriate to climb into bed with your mam and dad when you woke gasping for air or crying out for David Hasselhoff. And anyway, sometimes it was Pamela Anderson doing the rescuing and it all worked out fine in the end. But this wasn't California. No one was running to the rescue in slow-motion. This was the North Sea, and his body was about to have an early crack at the Boxing Day Dip.

The fear returned.

Rob panicked and closed his eyes. He tried to control his breathing, but that anxiety-reducing technique only really works on people who have a functional respiratory system. He *felt* like he was breathing. He knew the actions. In. Out. Blow. Suck. It was simple. Babies do it. *Bees do it. Even educated fleas do it!*

That was Cole Porter. Or was it Victoria Wood? He giggled madly and hummed to himself. His mind was in tatters. Thoughts of comedy shows and being home with the family flashed through his head—of Chinese food in foil trays, sitting on the floor watching Saturday night TV—but those happy memories were being pushed back by death, drowning, and Dalmatians with more colour than was strictly necessary. He grabbed the side of his head and groaned. *It can't be real!* he thought. *It can't be! It's all in my head!* But then another thought overrode the rest, something he couldn't deny… he had seen it with his own eyes. Zombies!

But weren't they just in movies and TV shows?

Rob fought the rising panic with images of the familiar—*Star Trek, Land of the Giants, The Darling Buds of May, Bottom, Kula Shaker at Middlesbrough Town Hall*—repeating them over and over in his head. Anything to bring him back from the edge.

He took a breath (sort of) then turned his mind to Arnold Rimmer from *Red Dwarf*. *Is it cold outside?* he thought to himself. *There's no bloody atmosphere at all!* He thought of rusty chains and seats that held him. There had been touch there. There had been contact.

If he could do it then, he could do it now.

Rob opened his eyes, looked at his body... and shoved. His hands, such as they were, hit his shambling body in the shoulder and turned it.

"Get in!" Rob cried in exultation. The zombie-him stumbled in the water and tried to turn, but Rob hit him again. It hurt. No, not hurt. It took... effort. He lifted his hands, staring in confusion as lights glistened through his palms and he realised they were the lights of the town.

"I'm Marty McFlying!" he gasped, but he had done it. His body ambled along the waterline, parallel to the sea, heading back towards town.

Rob was so relieved to have stopped his body going to a watery grave that he didn't see the inherent flaw in his plan. If he had given it some more thought he might have realised that sending a zombie in the direction of civilization probably wasn't the smartest move. But he didn't, and if he was about to, it didn't matter, because the phone in the pocket of his body started to ring.

Hand in my Pocket

Zombies follow their senses, such as they are. Sights and sounds draw them on, and they keep moving until more stimulus is found. It's a pretty simple system, but one that now, in the face of that classic Nokia ringtone pealing from the left pocket of a pair of jeans, meant Rob's zombie turned in slow shuffling circles like a dog with a tail fixation. To make the visual image even stranger, the ghost of Rob skipped after it while trying to exact a clumsy pickpocket. It was the roundabout all over again. Only without the nunchucks and violence.

"Come here, you git!"

Rob chased his body in a circle with one hand in the pocket. Well, he thought it was in the pocket, but it kept slipping back *through* the denim, or worse, *forward*. It was part pickpocket, part colonoscopy. Rob was growing tired, his form losing vibrancy as it faded, but he wanted that phone. He needed that phone. An image had crept into his mind, and he couldn't shake it. His mam's favourite movie. *Ghost*. There was a scene where Patrick Swayze typed his name on a computer. Imagine if he had a phone! That whole weird, possessing Whoopi Goldberg for a cuddle with Demi Moore thing would have been a bit different. If Rob could just get it, he could text. One hundred and forty characters or less.

Hi Mam, don't freak out. I'm dead. But I can still text. Lol.

He'd work on it.

The phone stopped ringing and the zombie stopped dancing. Rob stumbled to a halt, realising as he did that he was breathing heavily, his chest rising and falling, and he shook his head at how much that didn't make sense. He looked at his hands and gasped. He was vanishing quicker than Casper. There were so many thoughts and images and pop culture references floating through Rob's brain he wondered if this is what they meant when they said that life flashes before your eyes when you die.

Music, computer games and TV. *Great. The sum of all my parts.*

The zombie stood still, eyes staring straight ahead, unblinking, annoyingly handsome, the head twitching slightly at any small sound. Rob realised he might not get another chance and concentrated everything he had on getting his hands inside that pocket.

A passer-by giving this scene a quick glance through the thinning mist would see nothing more than a handsome young man standing on the beach, lost in thought. But one of those fortunate folk (or unfortunate, depending on your point of view) who have the second sight would see a faintly transparent, nearly identical young man concentrating hard on his own arse. With his tongue sticking out.

The fabric of the pocket moved. Rob held the breath he wasn't breathing and focused everything he had on his hand. He had the phone! It was right there between his fingers! He gripped and pulled. It rose in the pocket of the 501s and he cried out with hope and joy.

And then the beach exploded.

The Kids Aren't Alright

The sky erupted into bright orange flame, and it seemed as though the mist itself caught fire. Rob knew immediately what this was. He had lived in Redcar his whole life, and being so close to British Steel and ICI, the residents were well accustomed to the flare-offs from the vast factories, mills, and plants to the north of the town. Occasionally, the flare was so massive it turned the sky orange. It was mesmerising. It was biblical. It was as though the whole town had been Tango'd. During the day, the flare shone a new dawn. At night, the world glowed like the apocalypse.

Apt, considering.

As it was, the timely and expensive special effect caught the attention of Rob's zombie, who had no such lasting memory, and started the bemused creature on a stately march north. Rob lost his grip on the phone and fell over, swearing at the uncomprehending figure of his recently vacated body, who, he had to admit, was walking better. Even with a touch of swagger. The git.

Rob dusted himself down—ineffectually and completely unnecessarily—and gave chase.

And the world exploded again.

This time it was an actual explosion and not deserving of the dramatic gap caused by a chapter break.

There was a loud crack and a fizz as a green ball of fire shot over the sand, rocketed through Rob, and exploded behind him. The zombie turned to follow with all the reflexes of a hungover Sunday League goalkeeper and then another explosion caused it to turn again and stumble. The shots kept coming—the familiar scream and whine of fireworks kicking up showers of sparks and sand. Red. Green. Red. Green. There was laughter from the dunes. Dark figures huddled together, illuminated by the flicker and flash of someone trying to work a lighter. A flame caught; there was a fizz of sparks, more laughter and someone shouted.

"Fucking lob it!"

An object carved a graceful arc through the orange mist and landed at the feet of the zombie. Rob dove full stretch on his belly with confused thoughts of *Soldier Soldier* running through his mind and threw his hands over his head. When he realised the embarrassing futility, he quickly got back up. Nothing happened. If he still had the olfactory equipment necessary to make deductions, he would've picked up a strange metallic, rotten egg scent hanging in the mists. The object hissed and fizzed. The zombie turned in the sand, much to the amusement of the still partially hidden assailants, and then Rob caught sight of the missile. A coke can, wedged into the sand where it had landed at the zombie's feet.

The bastards! He knew this trick.

The can vibrated.

The zombie looked down.

The can exploded.

It rocketed skyward via the zombie's chin, felling Rob's body like a chopped tree. A tracksuit-clad gang of kids swaggered onto the beach as the zombie rose unsteadily and Rob raised his hands to push him out of the way, but then he stopped.

He thought about it.

Really thought about it.

He was already tired, already losing form, and he was angry. In fact, he was bloody furious. He hated people like this. People who didn't give a shit. People who got pleasure from hurting others. He watched as they approached and knew he should probably try to help, but then, would *they* help *him*? The moral implications of action versus inaction floated through his mind. Was not doing something the same as doing something? It wasn't *him* putting these unsuspecting twats in danger, not really, and if he did push the zombie away wouldn't they just chase it? And he was dead! At some point, moral responsibility has to slip away, right? Rob reached a decision.

He folded his arms across his chest and did absolutely nothing.

Four 'lads' appeared, passing around a bottle of White Lightning and laughing at what they thought was an old man knocked over by a 'banger bomb'. The ringleader swaggered closer and the zombie growled. Rob almost wavered but then the little scrote opened his mouth.

"Alright, yer fucking spacker! Give us yer wallet!"

Fuck it, Rob thought. *Que sera, sera.*

The zombie reached out for the young thug and the boy pushed his hands away, swearing at him, bouncing around on his heels in that way English kids do when they think they're being hard. The zombie was disorientated by the flare from the north, the hit from the coke can, and the noise caused by a pack of arrogant meerkats in matching tracksuits, but then the youths attacked *en masse,* and everything got a little messy.

The ringleader tried for a two-handed shove as his cronies veered in, but he didn't account for the dead weight of *rigor mortis,* and his weak little wrists nearly broke on the corpse. The zombie grabbed the side of the boy's head and squeezed, long fingers slipping into his ears. For a moment, the angry little pleb might have thought it was a classic 'wet willy' but as they dug deeper and the thumbs closed over his eyes, any and all thoughts were pushed aside by agony.

In much the same way a newborn child, if left unsupervised, will make its way to the breast, a zombie has an uncanny ability to find the nearest portal of entry. Rob's zombie found four. The boy screamed and screamed but the zombie lifted him and bit into his skull, opening a fifth. The screams turned into something else entirely.

The cronies didn't understand what was happening. All they saw was their friend being held by a strange man and so they didn't run in terror. Not yet. That was a mistake. The zombie dropped the first kid and grabbed one attacker by the throat and one by the arm. Teeth flashed in the night as screams filled the beach. Rob watched the fourth and final youth piss himself and run.

It was over in moments.

The first attacker lay twitching on the ground, a great bite out of his skull, blood soaking into the sand from his ears and eyes. The second fell, his throat ripped clean away. The third had copped a bite to the wrist and lay screaming next to the twitching bodies of his friends. There was blood everywhere, except on the zombie itself. Oh, there was some on his chin and lips, but a dark tongue poked from the mouth and soon took care of that.

Rob threw up.

Well, he tried.

Hedonism (Just Because You Feel Good)

The emotions were different. The thought processes different. Rob was still Rob, but much of what he now experienced was no longer chemical, no longer biological. It was memory. The disgusted reaction to the violence on the beach came from a *memory* of what it means to be disgusted. The churning in his ethereal stomach wasn't there, but that didn't matter because it *felt* like it was. Rob knew what he'd just witnessed was appalling—the stuff of nightmares, movies, and computer games—in that sense, it was much like the fear: instinctual and still very much part of who he was. Rob no longer had instincts brought about by biology, but he did have the ones he carried in his mind.

As he watched his old body gnawing on a piece of new brain the thought occurred to him that a significant aspect of a person's morality might depend on the physical nature of the human condition. It was, after all, proving to be much easier not to give a toss now that he was dead. But then, maybe that's because he had bigger things to worry about? Just because something feels good, didn't make it right, and just because he couldn't feel a damn thing didn't make it right either, right?

He paced back and forth. Should he have tried? Should he have cared? He looked at the two bodies on the beach. Sure, they were deadshit little scallies who had been quite happy to lob fireworks and mug someone, but did they deserve to die? Well, *he* didn't deserve to die but here we are, elbows deep in theology, horror movies and Iron Maiden album covers.

Two bodies.

The thought interrupted his musing. He looked down.

One.

Two.

Skull-less kid and throat-less kid. Pissy-pants kid had done a Road Runner and was long gone, but where was the one with the knackered wrist? Rob twisted and turned and saw a tell-tale stain tracing a straight run over the beach, a sticky Hansel and Gretel trail soaking into the sand. Further along, where the washed-up pebbles gathered in a pile against the old wooden sea fences, fresh blood glistened in the faint light. There was a glimmer of moisture on the concrete slope rising from the beach, and at the top, a scared kid desperately trying to reach the relative safety of the footpath.

Rob wasn't sure what to do. He wasn't sure if there was anything he *could* do. It wasn't like he could race after the boy and… what? Explain it was all a misunderstanding? Give him a damn good talking to about making better life choices?

By pure coincidence, and with no small sense of irony, Rob's body made the decision for him when the fleeing boy tripped and cried out. The zombie's eyes snapped up and locked on the young lad as he got to his feet, and even from this distance, Rob could see the terror and pain etched on the kid's face. He had to help. Of course he did. Violent scally or not, he was just a bairn.

Rob's zombie set off after the terrified child and Rob's ghost jogged in front. Right was right, and this was wrong.

"Hope you're happy now," he said to himself.

In the Meantime

The fleeing boy darted over the Stray and onto Coast Road, possibly hoping to flag down a car, but the town was deserted. The kid ran in panic and then stopped suddenly, crying out in shock, and not really knowing why. Rob did. He had run right through him. The ghost shouted at the boy, waving his arms in his face, screaming at him to run but the poor kid was frozen in fear, twisting and turning, clinging to the wound on his wrist. It dripped like a tap through shaking fingers.

"It's okay, it's okay," he sobbed, looking for help, but there was none. "It's not okay." The sky blazed and the mist magnified it, painting everything above the houses and trees a bright orange. The world burned and the kid bled and cried. Alone.

There was a noise then, like the groan your granny makes getting out of a chair—only with more teeth. Rob's zombie appeared from the mists like the Terminator himself. The young lad looked towards Zetland Park, perhaps thinking he could flee through the tennis courts and knock on a door to get help, but he didn't move, he just turned in small circles of wide-eyed terror.

"Run! You daft get!" Rob shouted. Even *he* was beginning to feel nervous about the approaching zombie. It wasn't just the *Silent Hill*-style mists it emerged from, it was the unrushed, steady, and above all, *patient* pace of the thing—the inevitability of death.

To really ratchet up the mounting tension (and the puddle on the floor) a grinding shriek shattered the night with an unerring sense of occasion. A gate opened.

The boy turned.

So did Rob.

So did Rob's zombie.

There were people—three of them.

The boy cried out, screaming in hope and pain. He clamped the wound with his free hand, blood everywhere, hot and sticky. He was pale, almost grey.

"Help me!" he called, and the newcomers turned. Rob watched as the last of the colour drained from the boy's face and the hope died.

It was the way they moved.

The stride, the shuffle, the new familiarity cutting through the kid's fear and pain. They stepped from the mists and Rob groaned. He recognised all three and it might have surprised him to know, so did the boy. He'd bought weed from the one in the middle just a few hours ago. But familiarity did not, in this instance, beget comfort, because Wayne Dickson's lips were missing. Both of them. His bright white teeth shone through the tattered mess in a clown-like grimace, a skeleton in a ragged human mask. One girl's mouth was drenched crimson, tatters of flesh hanging from her lips. The other had bloody chunks ripped from her shoulders. In the short look Rob got of the advancing threesome, he drew some pretty quick, and surprisingly accurate, conclusions.

* * *

It had been a good snog, albeit a toothy one, and the girl's friend had politely turned her back and lit another joint while they got on with it. Wayne had been buzzing—off his tits, in fact—and not entirely sure what had happened in the park. But that didn't matter, there was a warm and willing girl in his arms, and drugs in his veins, so he didn't give a monkey's.

The friend was just as happy. She had a joint and a Sony Discman in the pocket of her puffer jacket. She might act far older than she was, but she bloody loved The Spice Girls. The girl set the volume to maximum when the sounds got a little vigorous, which was fine; it just meant she never heard them come.

Wonderwall

The four zombies united in the middle of the road to the soundtrack of 'Who Do You Think You Are.'

The kid ran.[3]

He found no help at the nursing home on the corner; the residents too old, deaf, scared, or asleep to react to his frantic cries. He left bloody handprints on every window as he banged on the glass in weakening desperation but still no one came. Rob urged him on, encouraging him to keep moving, but the boy couldn't hear. He turned and leaned against the wall, breathing heavily. The zombies were on the roundabout now, struggling a little to get through the roses snagging at their feet, but still they came. They'd never give up. Rob watched as the kid closed his eyes, steeling himself to keep going but then a new noise broke the night, and everything changed. They all heard it. The rumble, hiss, and roar of a double-decker bus. The boy pushed himself off the wall and Rob ran back to the roundabout. The bus was coming along Granville Terrace, heading for the Coast Road, the headlights already washing the mists with yellow light. It was right there. The boy might make it!

The zombies turned as the bus came screaming around the corner. Rob stopped. Something was wrong. The driver didn't slow, and the giant metal beast roared as it mounted the kerb. It smashed through a reflective bollard and collected two zombies at full speed. Spice Girl vanished under the wheels and Wayne bounced off the windscreen with a slap. Rob didn't have time to

---

[3] It was probably The Spice Girls that pushed him over the edge.

move. His jaw dropped as the bus drove through him, and he marvelled at the amount of detail you can pick up in a short, dramatic, space of time.

The driver was dead. Sort of. His foot was wedged onto the accelerator and his newly reanimated hands held the wheel in a death grip as he flashed through Rob. Behind him, the bus was in chaos. A huddle on the back seats tried desperately to hold off an advancing mass of snapping and snarling bodies. Two teen girls, a man in a suit, and an old lady all screamed as the bus bounced and rose into the air. Rob, standing on the road, suddenly found his head level with the floor. There was a little dog; cowering behind a tartan shopping bag, but then it was gone. The bus passed through Rob quicker than a week-old curry.

He watched the great red vehicle bounce as it missed the turn, the second girl tumbling over the tarmac in its wake.

He watched Wayne slap into the wall of Zetland Park with a noise like a damp sock and somehow stick the landing.

And then he watched the bus smash into him.

There was no Hollywood explosion, no dramatic special effects, no last-second look of surprise on Wayne's face. He did snarl, but with half a face, that was a given. One second, he was there, the next; he was wearing a bus. The big red behemoth bucked as all four wheels rose then crashed back down, the wall somehow standing firm. Then, with the inevitability of drunken Jenga, the giant vehicle toppled and fell, crashing sideways to the road with a noise like thunder.

It was the coolest thing Rob had ever seen. *The wheels on the bus go round and round,* he thought as the echoes of the crash faded away to be replaced by the sound of screams and bangs. Smoke soon licked from beneath the bus to rise over the large rear window. There was movement in there. Slow at first then increasingly frantic. Eventually, though, the world returned to silence.

When Rob finally tore his eyes away, he found himself alone in an empty street. The boy was gone, but Spice Girl, somehow, was on her feet and heading into the darkness of Lord Street; the eerie, distorted warble of 'Wannabe' echoing from the walls as she faded into shadow.

Wannabe

Rob didn't run this time. What was the point? Spice Girl had been flattened by a double-decker bus and yet still got up and carried on as though nothing happened. Rob could barely touch things without feeling thin and stretched out, as substance-less as over-diluted school juice. What use could he possibly be? But then someone screamed. It was the boy. And he knew he had to try.

Once more, Rob found himself moving, the patient ghost trailing the inexorable zombie.

Lord Street was a long curve of dark brick walls and garage doors behind an unbroken line of tall, terraced houses. The meagre light of the streetlamps did next to nothing under the bright glow of the flare but the strange night cast odd shadows that stretched and reached across the street. Rob saw yellow, reflective eyes peering from between bins, watching him in shivering fear as he went. Bloody cats! He knew they were dodgy bastards! He jogged along the path, passing the net-curtained windows of people's front rooms. Television sets glowed blue and purple on the other side of the glass and he caught glimpses of people on their couches, oblivious to the chaos of the world outside. *Lethal Weapon* played in one house, adverts for Dime Bars in another, and *An Audience with Billy Connolly* in a third. He loved Billy Connolly. So did his parents. He wondered if they would be watching that right now, equally unaware that very soon their lives would change forever once they realised their son was dead.

Their son was dead.

That's me.

Rob stopped in shock just as the row of houses ended and the street opened into Fisherman's Square. It was a heavy thought to bear, but the sight before him was a good distraction. Rows of tractors and small fishing boats filled the square, all festooned with nets, pots, and the other accoutrements for those braving the North Sea. The strange shadows cast by the flaring chemical plant made the darkness beneath the vehicles move and writhe about. That in itself was creepy enough, but the sight of a bleeding boy swinging a long fishhook on a pole at three slathering zombies kind of took precedence. It was clear he was on his last legs. He wasn't swearing, he wasn't talking, he wasn't trying to reason with them. The boy cried as he swung and parried away clawing hands... fighting for his life to the soundtrack of a garbled Spice Girls song. The CD player had been half crushed beneath the bus, not enough to stop it working, but certainly damaged enough to ruin (depending on your point of view) the girl group's signature song.

The music got louder as Rob drew closer, magnified and carried on the mists. It sounded like a slow grunge cover of the hit single 'Wannabe,' and honestly, it was a lot better. Rob looked up at the wide-eyed boy and felt a wave of compassion that would have been far more useful twenty minutes ago. The young lad was doing a pretty decent job of holding off his attackers considering the gaping wound in his left wrist, but he was fading fast. The wound dripped. The kid thrust desperately at Spice Girl and caught her in the shoulder. She barely flinched as he pushed her back into the faint pool of light cast by the moisture-covered streetlamp. Rob got a good look at her and shuddered. Her bones were broken, her skin torn like ripped denim. Wide gashes with frayed edges revealed all those inner workings that work so much better when they are inner. And there was a tyre track on her face! An actual tyre track, like a sticker over the bonnet of a car. Rob was stunned. None of the injuries seemed to have slowed her down—apart from the odd bone catching on a fishing net. In that moment, he christened her Scary Spice, because, well, she was fucking terrifying.

The kid pulled back and then slammed the hook into her chest. It was a good hit, given strength by sheer terror, but Scary just snarled and pushed herself deeper onto the pole until it ripped through her back. The gruesome instrument burst into the night with the girl's dead heart pierced on the end like a pickled onion on a cocktail stick.

That was too much for the kid.

He sat down on a tackle box with a sound that could have been a laugh but probably wasn't. Scary Spice still pushed forward, but the pole wedged against the boat and all she could do was thrash and snarl over the gunwale.

'If you wanna…' Clunk. Clunk. Grunt.

Rob wouldn't have minded a little sit down himself at that point, but his own zombie had somehow managed to clamber onto the wheel-arch of the trailer and was now reaching into the boat from the other side. The remaining dead girl shuffled around to follow his lead. Rob swore to himself and climbed up. Then he swore *at* himself, but he didn't hear.

The kid was still alive, his breath coming in short, ragged gasps, and Rob knew he couldn't let the poor bugger be eaten. He positioned himself between his dead body and the living kid and concentrated. It was going to take a lot of effort to push this bloody thing off the trailer, but hopefully, he thought, it would give the young fella a chance.

* * *

It is probably worth a brief pause here to cover a few things. Yes, Rob's ghost did just climb into a boat and no, he did not fall through. Yet again, this is one of those metaphysical conundrums he simply hasn't had time to process, but that's not the important thing. The important thing is the kid. Specifically, his wrist. It's just a matter of time, right? Rob should know this. He's seen enough zombie movies and played enough computer games to know how it all works, but ask yourself a more important question, how rational would you be if your recently reanimated corpse caused a zombie outbreak in a small seaside town in the late nineties… and looked sexy while doing it?

Yeah, thought so. Stop being so judgemental and let the poor dead wannabe rock star get on with it. He's trying his best.

* * *

Rob's zombie leaned in with gnashing teeth and the kid begged for his mum. At that moment, the spirit of Rob felt something he would have previously called his heart lurch in what might once have been his chest. It was too much. Yes, the kid had been a twat. Yes, he was a firework-lobbing bully. Yes, he was dressed head to toe in a matching three-stripe tracksuit and dripping in Argos jewellery, but he was still a kid. He was still someone's son. No one deserved this.

Rob closed his eyes for a moment, opened them, and grabbed his own body by the shoulders.

It worked!

The steel-eyed zombie struggled but Rob had a good grip. He cried out at the effort, feeling a wave of nausea worse than a Red Stripe hangover ripple through him, and he offered up a prayer.

"Patrick Swayze, help me!"

Rob forced his body back, pushing himself across the boat. The legs hit the railing and the zombie toppled over the edge. Rob fell to the deck and groaned, gasping at the effort it had taken. It was far worse than climbing the rope in PE, and considering the movements he could hear below, probably just as useless. As he lay there, the other girl clambered up and fell inside the boat.

"Give me a break," he cried. Rob was fading fast, in every sense of the word, he could barely see his hands as he tried to raise them, and he felt a weariness in the core of his being. The orange light of the sky began to dim as the zombie girl reached for the kid but her searching fingers stopped and she turned away. Rob managed to tilt his head just in time to see the lips of the boy curl at the sides and his eyes snap open. They were like steel.

"Well… bollocks," Rob gasped.

And then it all went dark.

Faith

Rob woke—for want of a better word—in Vikki's car, completely alone apart from the blood stains and discarded drug paraphernalia. For a second, he thought it might all be a dream, and he sat completely still, hoping the world would somehow set itself right. Outside the car, the thick mists swirled slowly and patiently, waiting for him to get his shit together.

"What the fuck am I doing here?" Rob said, staring at the Jackson Pollock they'd made of the upholstery.

Eventually, he stepped from the vehicle and into the night. He glanced around the empty car park, feeling a nauseating sense of déjà vu. The bald man's car was there, still with the door open, but that was it. The surreal weather was certainly keeping people away. Far to the north, the flare stack stood out like dragon fire with the shivering silhouette of the town huddled beneath. His uncle had explained the big flares to him once. They happened when there was too much fuel and nothing to do with it. So, they set it on fire. It was dangerous, Uncle Mike said, and a massive waste of money, but bloody good fun.

As if embarrassed by the attention, the stack flickered and winked out in a sulk. Rob blinked and ran. Darkness settled over the town, and by the time he passed through the gates of the beach park, it carried all the hallmarks of a straight-to-VHS horror. A dead body on the roundabout, thick grey swirls of mist clinging to the picnic tables, and shadows everywhere. The only thing missing was the ominous creak of the lonely swing, but Rob didn't have time to stop and play. He had a dead body to find. He laughed then, struck the absurdity of the whole thing. This was a really shit version of *Stand by Me*.

Stand by Me.

Stephen King.

The Body. That's what the book was called, and here he was, trying to find his own. Rob started to hum as he jogged along the Stray, the reworded lyrics of a George Michael classic[4] appearing from the ether in that way songs have.

"I guess it would be nice if I could... find my body!"

Suddenly, new lights broke through the mist and the unmistakable red and blue of a racing police car appeared in a blaze of cinematic, fog-swirling glory. It screeched to a halt beside the stricken bus and the door was flung open. A lone bobby emerged ready for action, clearly living his *Lethal Weapon* Martin Riggs dreams. He smashed the rear window with his truncheon, no doubt thinking he was about to rescue those stuck inside, but Rob was close enough to see the eyes of the copper grow wide as reaching hands dragged him through the shattered glass. There was no scream, but there were plenty of other noises.

Rob ran on without looking, he didn't dare. It wasn't just the bus and the grisly horror inside, there was something deeply upsetting about the abandoned police car—the radio buzzing, the lights flashing, all that equipment designed to help people, now completely impotent. He ran past the Shoreline Nursing home with its bloody handprints and along Lord Street with its dazzling television sets. He broke into Fisherman's Square and went straight to the boat. Scary Spice was still there, wearing her heart on her sleeve, her body held in place by the long fishhook, and the other two were on the deck where he left them. Neither moved. They stood stock still, steely eyes gazing into the mist. Rob stepped forward, moving around the boat. He stopped. He looked up. He walked back through. Then he looked underneath. Then he swore.

One, two, three. Two girls and a chav... and no sign of Rob.

His body was gone.

---

[4] The Limp Bizkit version, obviously. This is Rob we're talking about.

A well of despair rose within the ghostly young man and he almost gave up beneath the iron gaze of the dead kids, but before he could get completely washed away in self-pity, a noise he had not been expecting broke the stillness and interrupted his thoughts. The rolling bells of St Peter's Church chimed over the rooftops and bounced from the buildings in their familiar telling of the hour. It was a sound he normally loved, but right then it filled him with anger.

For whom the bell tolls.

His dad's favourite song. Religion again. Faith again. Weren't they supposed to be the experts in all this? Weren't they supposed to have answers?

As the peal subsided into echo and single chimes rang out to mark the time, Rob shook himself off (metaphorically speaking) and made up his mind. The anger was still there, but he was going to direct it. What was it his old man always said? 'Go straight to the top, son. If you have a problem, go see the man in charge.'

He was going to go see the man in charge.

He was going to church.

Hurry Up and Wait

If Rob knew what an absolute bloody disaster it was going to be just to make it the few hundred yards up the road to St Peter's, he might not have bothered, but he was dead, and his body had gone for a Burton, what else did he have to do? Best laid plans and all that.

It was the bells.

They drew the zombies as much as they drew Rob. They turned towards the sound and set off, but it all went tits up almost immediately. The two on the boat knocked into the low gunwale and fell over the edge, hitting the ground like bags of wet cement, while behind them, Scary Spice continued in her efforts to become a walking kebab. The fishhook had developed a layer of gristle usually only familiar to murderers and incompetent surgeons. By the time the bells stopped at ten and the echoes died away, the zombies had made it to their feet and were picking their way through the boats with a resigned Rob tagging along.

It was a solid ten minutes before the two walking corpses even made it to the edge of the car park, and when they did, they were confronted by yet another seemingly insurmountable obstacle... a low chain-link fence. This was enough, it seemed, to defeat even the most determined of the mortally challenged. Rob decided to have a little sit down and slumped on the moist ground like a kid on assembly, cross-legged and miserable... but oddly fascinated. It was like watching two drunk toddlers trying to get through a baby gate. No matter how much they tried, they just couldn't work it out. Neither fell, but they spent a small eternity staring blankly at the chain and slowly lifting one foot after the other. Rob never thought he'd be in a situation where he'd cheer on a zombie but he almost clapped when the dead scally kid finally made it over the chain and trotted forward.

The girl still struggled and for a moment Rob thought about just giving her a shove to get the party moving, but he didn't want to risk waking up two miles away again. He was complete now, recharged, and full colour. He supposed the wait had done him good but now the boy shuffled away, and the girl was still stuck. Rob got to his feet again. It was like herding cats. He looked from one to the other, trying to decide what to do, and was just about to race after the boy when the girl tripped.

She hit the concrete with such a slap that Rob burst out laughing. He couldn't help it. Her shoe caught in the chain, and she went over like Del Boy falling through the bar. A perfect comedy belly flop.

He stopped laughing when her foot came off.

It made a noise like a shucked mussel and hung from the chain by the laces of her black Kickers, the little red tag on the sole flashing as it spun.

"Oh, come on!" Rob said, "how the hell did that happen? You've only been dead five minutes!" But the girl didn't care about sense or logic or any of that stuff. She was free. She rose on the stump and kept going, leaving red and black potato prints on the road as she shuffled along. Rob threw his hands in the air.

The girl tried to follow the young boy, but the lack of a foot caused her to drift like a one-legged duck and she was pulled inexorably towards the dark open maw of the automated car wash. The boy was close to The Citz now—the Redcar Citizens Priory Club—a square, red-brick pub on the corner of William Street. It was the last stop before the church and Rob realised with a sinking sensation that the zombies would never make it past the golden windows to the church beyond. There would be too much noise, too many drinkers, too many people playing pool. Certainly more than enough life to distract a curious carnivorous cadaver. He was just about to run after the kid when the machines in the car wash kicked into gear and the sinking feeling well and truly sank.

Rob knew full well what he would see before he got there, but sometimes it's nice to be wrong.

He did *not* see the zombie girl get a lovely buffing from the automated rollers, and neither did he witness her receive a comedic shower and come out all squeaky clean and blood-free fresh.

Instead, he watched in dawning horror as she was ripped limb from limb.

The roller descended, scooped the girl up, and lifted her to the ceiling, where a flailing arm was caught in the gears. The machine groaned under the strain and started to smoke; the whole thing seemed to shake until suddenly it gave way. Or rather, *she* did. The poor dead girl was torn in two… and three… and four. Black sludge rained on the ground, and *then* the rollers started to spin. Water sprayed and soap foamed, and for a moment, Rob lost track of the girl as she tumbled around like a teddy in a washing machine. Then 'bits' started to fly out into the night, landing with heavy, wet splats on the road.

Rob ducked as a hand whizzed past him and stuck to the rear window of a Ford Escort like the world's shittest Garfield toy.

Then it got worse.

The girl's head shot towards him—mouth open, tongue out.

Time slowed.

Well, it didn't, but you get the point.

The broken teeth bore down on Rob, and he froze. The steely eyes of the dead girl closed, and for one horrible moment, his mind flashed back to the first real kiss he'd ever had. Year six. Mungle Jungle. Behind the ball pool. He had been so nervous. Which way should he tilt his nose? How long was it supposed to last? How wide should he open his mouth? As first kisses go, it wasn't bad, certainly deserving more honour than to dance in his memories while the severed head of a dead girl passed through his face with eyes closed and tongue out.

Rob is dead, let's be clear, he has no sense of taste or smell, and very little of touch, but a decapitated head going the extra eighty to your twenty is a bit much. I think we can forgive him for having a little sit down as the head rolled to a stop beneath a tractor. It's just a shame this meant he didn't see the approaching gang of zombies shuffling their way towards the pub.

The Beautiful People

The nomenclature in that final line might not be entirely accurate and there may even be purists who are frustrated at the substitution of "gang" for "horde." But the truth is, there aren't enough zombies to make a horde. Not yet. The shuffling group had recruited a police officer, however, and he still held his truncheon as he walked at the front of them all, so that was kind of cool.

The dead made a strange noise as they walked towards, and in some cases through, the ghost of Rob. It was an unnerving susurrus of shuffling, groaning, moaning, and escaping gasses. Think cicadas on a warm evening in a beautiful foreign country, except it wasn't cicadas, it wasn't warm, and it wasn't that pretty. Either way, it was enough for Rob to lift his head and get back to his feet. Death really wasn't working out the way he thought. At the very least he had hoped for a little guidance, perhaps even a Pratchett-esque anthropomorphic personification to point him in the right direction, but he was alone. He was going to have to figure this one out for himself.

Rob moved through the group in search of the young kid, catching sight of him outside The Citz—the tracksuit-clad form illuminated by pools of light cast by the wide windows. He was about a hundred metres away, just a black silhouette in a mist-shrouded street, but Rob watched as a man stepped from the building and the boy veered towards him. Rob sped up, rushing *through* the crowd and then breaking into a run. He caught the pair just as the boy bit the man on the hand. A lit cigarette fell to the floor in a shower of sparks and the man punched the boy in the side of the head. It was a good hit. The kid dropped like, well, like a kid who had been punched in the side of the head by a grown man. He groaned, his mouth full of blood, his lips moving. The older fella spat.

"Little twat!" he snapped and turned away, tucking his hand into his armpit. He fumbled for a key and opened the hairdresser's next door to the club, flicking the light on and walking inside. He crossed the floor to the sink, blood dripping all over the black and white tiles.

Rob followed. He was beginning to think he might be just as bad as the zombies—not bitey by any means, but still apt to trail after anything that grabbed his attention. The lights in the barbershop were bright and welcoming, whereas the streets outside were creepy and full of dead people. At the very least, the familiarity was comforting. It didn't last long. The boy followed them into the shop, bumping against the door as he entered. The man spun around.

"You want more, do you, you rabid little shitbag? Well, I'll teach you to go around biting people. Come here." The hairdresser wrapped a towel around his bleeding hand and stepped angrily towards the boy, entirely failing to see the pool of blood on a black tile. His feet flicked out in a way that might have been funny if this were any other situation, and he hit the floor with a smack. The zombie dropped to his knees, stuck his thumb in the hairdresser's groaning mouth before he could move, and pulled. The man's eyes widened in shock, then pain, then terror as the side of his face was ripped away and the boy stuffed the grisly mess into his mouth.[5]

The stricken hairdresser thrashed on the floor, knocking the boy aside and looking up as a policeman walked into the shop. The series of emotions on what remained of his face swung swiftly from painful hope to mortal dread when the policeman's own injuries and matching steely-eyed gaze became clear in the bright lights, and he wasn't alone.

The hairdresser had never believed in zombies, and this was a particularly shit way to find out he was wrong. Seeing the hope vanish in the man's eyes as the shop filled with shuffling creatures was too much for Rob. There

---

[5] Rob had eaten pig cheeks once. It was delicious. He didn't think this would be the same.

was nothing he could do to help, but he didn't have to stand and watch. He carefully picked his way outside, stepping over feeding bodies and thrashing limbs, apologising as he went.

"Excuse me. Sorry. Pardon me."

In the end, there were too many bodies in the way, they crowded in, ripping the old door from the hinges, and Rob had to walk through them. But anything was better than watching the short back and sides currently being received by the hairdresser. Hearing it was bad enough. The screams lasted far longer than he hoped, and he stumbled onto the footpath with something resembling a sigh of relief.

The street was empty.

All the zombies had somehow crowded into the man's shop, and as the last muffled cries drowned in blood and pain, Rob could almost kid himself that the world was normal.

Almost.

Not all the zombies were in the hairdressers. One was next door. On his knees in the foyer of The Citz, feeding. Polished boots kicked beneath a small desk and Rob had the unnerving experience of watching himself eat. The noises were even more disturbing than the ones from the hairdressers. The unmistakable sound of slurping, like a kid struggling with a McDonald's milkshake, echoed from the foyer, and Rob couldn't help but take a closer look.

There was surprisingly little blood.

And surprisingly little bouncer.

The mouth was there, but the ears and nose were gone. Even the eyes were missing—well, one of them was. There was another slurp, and the other followed. Rob watched as his body chewed thoughtfully, then swallowed. The dead body ran the back of its hand across its mouth and burped. It was a habit Rob's mam told him repeatedly to stop, and yet here he was, still doing it after death. Rob stood in open-mouthed shock. Perhaps it was still him, somewhere? Deep down? Maybe he could come back?

The zombie stood up, groaned, bumped into the desk, and *then* things got weird.

The Bartender and the Thief

It started with angry shouts from inside the bar and a dark figure growing more distinct as it ran towards the frosted glass. The door flew open, and a wild-eyed young man in grey tracksuit pants and a bright orange Ben Sherman shirt made a run for it. He didn't get far. He ran right into a zombie. The dead Rob lunged as if to take a bite but then changed its mind and dropped the mouth away at the last moment. By all the laws of biology, gravity and probably physics, if the mouth drops, the forehead follows. Thus, it happened that Rob's zombie delivered the single most precise and devastating headbutt since Russ Abbott's CU Jimmy. The fleeing lad's nose exploded across his face, and he staggered back into the waiting arms of the barman who had been giving chase.

"Got ya! Ya thieving twat! No one steals beer from me. Thanks, mate," the barman said with a nod to Rob. "Give me a second and I'll buy you a pint."

The bartender and the thief grappled on the steps of the club, but it was a foregone conclusion. The bleeding lad was already disorientated, and the barman had him by the collar of his big shiny shirt—XXL on a skinny frame; plenty of fabric to get a hold of. The other fist rained punches into the already mangled nose before he simply let go.

"Hope the beer was worth it, you bell end," the barman snapped as the kid hit the pavement. "Robbing the locals. No class."

The kid scrambled to his feet and ran away, completely unaware of just how lucky he was. The barman watched him go, then looked around. "Where the fuck is Tony?", he said.[6] The street was empty, but the lights were on next door and shadows moved inside. He shrugged. Probably having another fag break. He'd bollock him later.

The man turned to go back up the steps when something caught his eye. He paused for a moment and looked at Rob, but the zombie had his back to him, staring at the pub's door.

"Here we go," the ghost muttered and waited for the inevitable scream at the discovered body, but it didn't come. Instead, the man bent down, picked something up, quickly stuffed it in his back pocket, and jogged up the steps to slap the zombie on the back.

"Do I know you, mate?" he said. "Here, let me buy you a drink."

Rob was gobsmacked. All he could do was watch as the two figures disappeared into the pub and the frosted glass door closed behind them. He looked from the booted feet to the door and back to the feet. Then he shrugged and followed.

* * *

It is worth noting here that the door didn't close all the way. Not exactly. It was a damp night. It needed a little shove for the latch to take. It's a bugger really because zombies are useless at locks.

* * *

A zombie, a ghost and an unscrupulous publican walk into a bar. There isn't a punchline. It's just what happened. The barman directed Rob's zombie to one of the vacant stools and ducked behind the hatch to pour him the promised pint. Ghost Rob watched on, taking it all in, a little mesmerised by the whole scenario. *Why was he just standing there? Why wasn't he attacking people? Was he full? Did zombies have eyes bigger than their bellies? What if they'd just eaten*

[6] Nearly every bouncer in the north of England in the '90s was called Tony. No one knows why. It probably had something to do with predestination… if you believe in that sort of thing.

someone else's eyes?

Rob had no idea what the hell was going on, but he saw the barman pull something from his back pocket and place it under the till, so he wandered through the bar to get a closer look.

"Thieving git!"

There it was. Rob's own phone. Next to a cricket bat and a pack of Regal King Size. He tried to poke it but failed. It was hard to concentrate with the barman walking through him all the time. Rob swore and looked around. The Citz was an open-plan pub with a few plaster pillars propping up the Artex ceiling. Square tables and seats with faded red fabric made a clustered chequerboard, and the worn carpet gave way to Lino near the pool tables. People laughed and smoked in groups or sat alone, nursing pints of brown beer or golden lager. Rob hadn't been in many pubs that weren't family restaurants, but this didn't exactly fit the same mould as The Lion Inn, or the Cross Keys over in Guisborough. Honestly, it looked more like a school hall.

Rob looked at his handsome ex-body standing at the bar, cool as you like, as if he belonged, and yet again the unfairness of the whole situation washed over him.

"Git," he said.

The barman noticed Rob wasn't drinking and moved closer, wiping his hands on a cloth so filthy all it did was trade grime for grime.

"You okay, mate?" he asked. The zombie turned his head at the sound and nodded. Rob wasn't expecting that. Not at all. He moved closer and the faint glimmer of hope sparked up once more. Did he just respond? Was there some semblance of life there? If there was, then… perhaps?

Perhaps what? He'd been outside his body for at least an hour. He wasn't sure a defibrillator would do the trick.

"I'm Dave, by the way. Thanks for stopping that wanker."

The zombie stared at Dave. If anything was going on behind those gun-metal eyes, it was hard to say, but the gaze sent a splinter of ice down the barman's spine. He shivered then laughed it off.

"Bloody hell! I feel like someone just walked over my grave. Here, if you don't want lager, I can get you something different. Beer man, are you? Smiths or Boddingtons? I bet you like Bodies."

The barman replaced the lager with a creamy-headed pint and tossed the towel onto the bar.

"Here," he said, "use that to clean your face. You got a bit of that lad's blood on you when you nutted him."

The zombie remained silent and there must have been something in the look that concerned the barman. He called one of the women over and whispered in her ear.

"Here, what's wrong with this lad? Is he in shock?"

"Jesus, Dave! Do you know who that is?" the woman said, her face splitting into a wide grin as she finished her seventh cheeky shot of tequila. She was in her early thirties and hanging on desperately to her twenties. The hair, make-up and nails were a testament to effort. She was beautiful but fighting hard to be younger. She crossed around the bar and laid her arm on Rob's shoulder, with only the slightest stumble. The zombie turned towards her, his mouth open, it might have been a smile, it might have been a snarl, either way, the woman saw what she wanted to see. "This young lad was on TV last week," she beamed. "*Stars in Their Eyes.* He sang that song, Dave. You know the one. The Nirvana song. You were brilliant," she said to Rob. "He's a proper celeb now, Dave. You should get him to play a few songs. Would you do that, love? Would you play some songs for us?"

Fucking hell! Rob thought. *He's even getting gigs!*

"What do you think, lad?" Dave asked, pointing to a small stage in the corner of the room. The zombie turned to look where he was pointing. "I've got the equipment and there's a guitar out the back. A couple of songs to end the night? You can drink for free."

"Come on, love," the woman said. She hadn't taken her hand off Rob's shoulder, and now it slipped to his arm. "Janice will look after you. Let's get you cleaned up." She took Rob by the hand and led him away. Dave laughed and shook his head, taking the untouched pint and drinking it himself.

"Poor lad doesn't stand a chance," he said, sucking the foam from his lip as he watched Janice usher Rob into the back room and close the door. "She'll eat him alive."

Dave finished the drink in one go and then turned to one of his regulars. "Bit of music tonight, Bill. Spread the word. Got a TV star who wants to play a few songs."

It didn't seem to bother either Dave or Janice that Rob hadn't said a word. Dave was thinking of the advertising and the potential story in *The Evening Gazette*, perhaps even a bit on ITV, but Janice was thinking something else entirely. She made it pretty clear what was on her mind when she guided the pliable young man to the back room. For the ghost Rob, who had drifted through the walls to see what the hell was going on, it was like watching a dream. That was him. That was his body. That was Rob. But he watched, detached, as Janice used a wet cloth to clean his face. The two figures locked eyes and Rob had absolutely no idea what Janice was seeing in that grey gaze, but it certainly wasn't fear that he might bite her face off. She cleaned his neck with a tender touch, pulling his black t-shirt down a little to wipe the cloth over his chest. Rob growled—or groaned; ghost Rob wasn't sure which—but Janice was. She smiled, her eyes wide, and lifted his shirt, dropping the cloth and placing her hands on his chest.

"Were you nervous?" she breathed, her lips close to his neck as she moved in. "When you were on TV, were you nervous? Do you get nervous before you perform?" She kissed him on the neck and one of them groaned. Despite all the evidence to suggest it was no longer possible, Rob felt the warm prickle of embarrassment flush over his cheeks, but it was like *You've Been Framed*, he just couldn't look away. "Are you nervous now?" Janice asked, leaning back a little and running her nails down Rob's stomach, she stopped at the top of his jeans and then gripped the waist, curling her fingers over and pulling Rob closer. "I can help you relax," she said.

"What. The. Fuck," Rob said. "This has got to be hell. I can't... he's not... she... Ah, fuck it." He turned his back on them and walked through the wall.

Dave had moved a few tables away from the stage, and there was an electric guitar and a fairly decent sound system waiting behind the mic. The barman made phone calls while another member of staff served, and there was a buzz about the place now that wasn't there before.

Well, Rob thought, *that's all going to change if the zombie suddenly has an appetite again.*

The eating thing didn't make sense. He just couldn't wrap his head around it, but then, everything Rob knew about zombies came from movies, so he wasn't exactly sure about anything. Did it have to be human flesh? Did they get full? In one of the old bootleg films he watched as a kid, the zombies only ate brains. In another, an old black-and-white one, they ripped a woman apart and sat under a tree to have a little snack. That one stuck with him more than the others. It was the normality of the thing—a zombie picnic. He would have shuddered if he could.

The door to the back room opened and to Rob's surprise, both his body and Janice stepped out. Janice tucked a strand of hair behind her ear and once more led Rob by the hand, a strange smile on her face. A few more buttons on the top of her already low-cut blouse were undone, revealing the curve of her breasts and a shiny black bra. *Page 57. Empire Stores catalogue*, Rob thought, and hated himself for it. Janice took Rob to the stage and lifted the guitar over his shoulder. She patted him on the side of the face and turned to the watching room. Only then did she fix her shirt, slowly, and with her bottom lip held delicately between her teeth.

Dave strode over and took the mic.

"Christ, woman," he said, and then turned to the pub. "Call your friends, let them know. The Citz is playing host to television's very own local star and good friend to the club, Robbie Neville!" (He'd looked up his name in the paper). He clapped. Janice clapped and cheered. The crowd did the same and the ghost of Rob swore to himself as his body stood on the stage looking every inch a rock star. A dead rock star, but a rock star all the same. The applause died away and there was an expectant hush.

And then the show began.

Firestarter

Rob had no idea some of his rambling thoughts regarding the nature of the undead were damn close to the truth, but when the press of zombies burst through the door, they offered plenty of opportunities for analysis. His own body had fed remarkably well on the corpse of Big Tony, only stopping when it was literally full, but the group in the hairdressers had to share the barber's meagre offering and there simply wasn't enough to go around. They stumbled into the street looking for dessert just as Dave sound-checked the electric guitar with the only tune he knew.[7] It drew the zombies up the stairs and through the unlocked door like goths to a graveyard, covered in blood and very much ready for a bar snack.

The dead are much the same as the living when it comes to instinct. They, like us, are driven by some pretty basic needs—primarily, to survive. For most of the human race, that means finding a decent meal and someone to have babies with. For the living dead on this one night in Redcar, it meant finding warm hosts to pass on infectious spores. But you know what it's like when you eat something tasty: once you pop, you can't stop.

If you could look inside, you'd see it: the fungus, the spores, clambering all over the hypothalamus and not giving it a chance. But you can't. What you *can* see is the half-devoured, reanimated corpse of Big Tony biting through the neck of old Bob, who had just put his hat on because he couldn't be doing with this new-fangled racket they call music nowadays. If you want to look

---

[7] 'Smoke on the Water' by Deep Purple, but then, you knew that, didn't you?

at it positively, at least he didn't have to, but then, no one did. The zombies swarmed over the tables and three more people were ripped apart before anyone could work out it wasn't a fancy-dress prank by one of the local football clubs. There were screams and cries of terror as the reality of the unnatural danger sank in. But since the government had cracked down on football hooliganism, there were also a few lads just itching for a fight, and they rallied with remarkable speed (and one or two smiley-faced pills). Pool cues snapped over heads and bottles broke on tables. Shouts of "Stitch that, ya bastard" and other such contemporary equivalents of *Henry V's* "Once more unto the breach," lifted the rafters and the fighting spirit of the Burberry-clad locals. Dave mounted the bar, swinging his cricket bat towards anything that moved, while Janice stood behind him, lobbing bottles of Stella at anything that snarled.

"Not the expensive stuff!" Dave shouted, taking the policeman in the face with a crisp reverse sweep into the pickled eggs. "Throw the Bacardi Breezers! They're out of date anyway!"

Janice flung open the fridge and got to work. She had a good arm and a great aim. Colourful explosions of green, yellow, and red decorated the air as the alcopops smashed against the dead and one lad called Frank who always pissed her off.

The zombies were all inside now and the fight got desperate. Rob moved to the stage where his body still stood, guitar in hand, looking annoyingly cool while the world around him turned to shit.

"This is your fault," Rob said. "You started all this." His body didn't answer, but the lips lifted in a slight snarl, and he lurched forward as two zombies ripped the entrails from a screaming woman. The guts looked like a string of sausages and the snarling ghouls stuffed a long line into their mouths, munching away as the woman slowly died. Their lips met over the table in a way Disney clearly didn't have in mind when they made *Lady and the Tramp*.

A loud and discordant injection of grunge suddenly shattered the room as Rob's zombie moved and his hand crashed against the strings of the electric guitar. It was a far cry from Dave's garbled rendition of 'Smoke on the Water', but even Rob had to admit it sounded pretty bloody good. For a moment, the zombies stopped and turned towards the stage, and the survivors legged it.

They raced for the door, overturning tables and throwing chairs as they went. It's all well and good being a rock-hard footy hooligan with a reputation for mindless violence and never backing down in the terraces, but throwing a solid head-butt counts for bugger all when your opponent wants to gnaw a chunk out of your face. The abrupt power chords faded into a screech of feedback, but the distraction was enough; the surviving humans made a bolt for it and piled into the street.

Dave and Janice suddenly found themselves alone in a bar full of slathering, mindless simpletons, which was a fairly standard Saturday night by all accounts. Dave reached down and pulled Janice onto the bar. She stood beside him between the Guinness taps, brandishing a bottle of blue WKD in one hand and a bottle of port in the other.

"What are you going to do with those?" Dave asked, the first strained tones of the terrified finally breaking through the false bravado.

"I'm going to give these fuckers a Cheeky Vimto and get the hell out of here," Janice snarled.

"Fuck it," Dave snapped. "I've got insurance. Pass the Absinthe."

Janice grabbed the green bottle. Dave took a swig then smashed it in the face of a snarling regular. He reached into his pocket, took Janice by the hand, and flicked his lighter onto the bar before leaping into the fray.

If it makes you feel better to imagine that Dave and Janice survived and went on to live long and happy lives taking every zombie documentary job and reality TV gig they could lay their hands on, then imagine away. The truth is, we just don't know. Our story follows Rob (both of them) and right now they are heading towards the exit. It took a few goes for the zombie to get going as he was somewhat hindered by the guitar, but after a few mindless drives forward, the strap gave way and the hapless instrument fell to the floor with a crash that blasted through the amplifiers and reverberated around the room.

As the echoes of the stricken instrument faded into the screams and groans of a full-blown zombie outbreak, Rob and his body stumbled down the steps to catch a breath of fresh air.

Losing My Religion

Neither Rob nor Rob needed fresh air, but it's a nice little segue to the scene outside the bar—which was not unlike most Saturday nights at 11 pm—except for the flames licking at the windows. The street was full of dumbstruck drunks wondering what the hell to do now they were outside.

This night was a little different, however, this night contained no small amount of mortal dread and supernatural terror, so when the bells of St Peter's rang last orders, the terrified masses raced towards the apparent safety of the large gothic church. Normally, the gravestones and dark shadows of the transept were handy places to take a piss or cop a feel, but now, they were sanctuary.

"In here!" a skinhead shouted, taking charge of the situation with fear-induced thoughts of *Bravo Two Zero* rattling around his head and no small amount of ecstasy. When it's the only book you've read since *See Spot Run* and you read it every night, it has an impact. Fair play to the lad, but the over-enthusiastic, "go go go!" might have been a bit much. He kicked the door open, not quite registering that it was unlocked anyway, and the terrified mass followed him into the peaceful solitude of an old Anglican church whose priest and bell-ringers were just about to pack up for the night. The self-appointed sergeant slammed the door behind them and dragged a wooden shelf over, wedging it in place. Alpha Course pamphlets scattered all over the floor, and in the silence that followed, Skinhead's momentary courage deserted him.

"They were fucking dead!" he cried, tears streaking his face.

"I say, what is happening?" the priest stammered. He was far too young to say "I say" but now isn't the time for classism. The skinhead looked at the young man with something approaching desperation.

"We need you, Father. The dead… they're fucking dead!"

"Excuse me?"

The people fell amongst the pews and there was much wailing and gnashing of teeth. The priest took it all in and Lo, he bloody loved it! This was what it was all about. He'd seen *Stigmata*. He'd seen *End of Days* and *The Omen*. That's what he was looking for when he signed up. Real shit! Not coffee mornings, empty Sundays, and never-ending funerals. He wanted *The Exorcist* and *Preacher* comics, not *Father Ted* and *The Vicar of Dibley*!

There was a crash on the door, and everyone screamed, then looked at him… the skinhead included. They *all* looked at him. He beamed and straightened his dog collar. The people were frightened, and they needed guidance. A shepherd. He saw it all.

What he couldn't see was the ghost of Rob, who had just floated through the font and felt a little tickle, but that didn't matter. The priest was twenty-nine years old. He was from the Home Counties. This was his first placement after seminary, and finally, God had come up with the goods.[8]

"Fear not, my children," he intoned in a voice that definitely marked him as a dickhead rather than a saviour, but he didn't care. He was swept up in a spiritual fervour far more intoxicating than ringing a bloody bell. Scratches and bangs started on the main doors, and he moved towards them without a thought of fear in his tiny little mind. Priests don't get hurt. Not in England anyway. He pulled the shelf aside in a spiritual daze and yanked open the door. Rob watched in shock as the young man stepped outside and opened his arms as if to embrace the masses.

"My chil—" he said, but got no further than the fourth letter before Rob's zombie ripped his throat out. He was hungry again.

---

[8] He was also high as a kite on cough syrup but that's neither here nor there.

* * *

Have you ever heard someone being eaten? No, of course not, and sitting on the couch next to your mam while she tucks into a Chinese takeout just isn't the same. It's not the sound of eating that's the problem, it's when the food cries *while being eaten* that really messes with your head. The group inside the church cowered in the pews and tried not to breathe. Churches are quiet at the best of times, but when zombies are scratching at the doors or quite literally taking communion from a dead priest, you could hear a fish fart in the font.

"Why did he do that?" a lady whispered, her voice laden with fear and snot. "Why did he just go out the door like that?"

"Shhh, keep your voice down!"

"I don't need to keep my voice down, they can't get in. This is holy ground. He shouldn't have gone outside."

"What do you mean, holy ground?"

"It's a bloody church, innit? Holy. Stands to reason."

"Yeah, she's right. You get sanctuary in a church."

"What's that?"

"Not sure, I think it's a small room at the back. I remember colouring it in in RE."

"Yeah, I did that lesson too. It's up there, near the altar where the cross and stuff is."

"That's an apse."

"Isn't that a snake?"

"No, *sanctuary*! You get sanctuary in a church. Safety. People aren't allowed to touch you."

"Except for the bloody priests."

"... pretty sure it's a snake..."

"Wrong religion."

"They're all the same, mate."

"... Cleopatra got bit by one..."

"What I mean is, no one can come inside the church if you claim sanctuary."

"... on her tit..."

"How do you claim sanctuary?"

"Don't know. Pray?"

"Will you all please be quiet!"

Drunk people can't whisper so the impromptu theological debate echoed around the vast Nave,[9] throwing their words back from the vaulted ceiling. The terrified group fell into silence and listened to the scratching at the door. Somehow, it was worse than the screams.

Some deep racial memory of steeped-in Anglicanism filtered to the surface of the terrified group, and they shuffled deeper into the dark building, through the chancel, to the safety of the altar, knowing instinctively that the further they went, the closer they came to God (or something like that anyway). They huddled together on the other side of the cloth-covered table and listened.

"What are they?"

"Smackheads."

"What?"

"It'll be some new drug. They've all been glue-sniffing or something."

"I've never seen any drugs make people do that! It's like they didn't give a shit about anything. Like they couldn't feel pain."

"One girl had her shirt off," tutted an older lady, proving we all focus on our own things. "Can she not feel the cold? It's brass monkeys out there."

"Probably a Geordie."

"Come again?"

"You've not been out in Newcastle for a while have you, pet?"

"You're suddenly very quiet. Wasn't this your idea?"

All heads turned to the skinhead who had led them to the safety of the church in the first place. He sat hugging his knees in the corner, desperately trying to think what Andy McNab would do. He looked up. Nothing in his life had prepared him for this and his eyes betrayed the fear. People looked away. Skinhead guy was struggling. He loved reading about war, he loved war movies, he wore camouflage pants and dog tags when he did the big shop

---

[9] The biggest bit. Always a bugger to colour-in if your felt-tip was running out.

for his mam, but this wasn't what he expected at all. He looked to the floor.

"I think we should pray," he said.

To his surprise, no one laughed. They were all too scared and confused. They were in a church—most of them for the first time since school—and prayer seemed like the right thing to do. A few closed their eyes and some even steepled their hands in front of their chests. One fella crossed himself, though his mumbled, "spectacles, testicles, wallet and watch," kind of ruined the solemnity. They all waited in expectant silence.

"Does anyone know any prayers?" a young lad in a matching Kangol tracksuit asked. He fiddled nervously with the poppers on the side of his leg, unbuttoning and buttoning the clasps. His dad had laughed when he bought them, but they saved his life tonight when a searching hand reached for him beneath a table. The poppers did what they do and gave him just enough time to pull his leg away from snapping teeth. The thought of that blood-filled mouth made him shudder. He felt the hot shame of tears streak down his face, but no one said anything.

Rob watched it all with detached fascination. There was no God here, no answers, just terrified people looking for hope.

"There's the 'Our Father,'" a young woman said.

"How's that go?"

"Our father who did art… something, something. Sorry, I don't know." She too, began to cry.

"What about hymns? They're the same, aren't they? Can anyone remember any hymns?"

Quietly, softly, Andy McNab began to sing as memories of sitting cross-legged in school assembly came flooding back. He started slowly, his voice low and nervous as he pictured the words emblazoned on the school wall by the light of the overhead projector.

"Dance then, wherever you may be, I am the Lord of the dance settee. And I'll—"

"The Lord of the what?"

"The Lord of the dance settee."

"What's a dance settee?"

"Dunno. There's probably one in here somewhere."

"I think it's Lord of the dance *said he*."

"Well, I always sung dance settee."

"Let's try another."

"What's that one about the jet planes meeting in the air? I loved that one."

"Yeah, that's a banger."

"Go on then."

Rob could barely contain himself as he watched a ragtag group of shivering drunks relive the glory days of their childhood. Skinhead even closed his eyes as he sang, but it floundered pretty quickly when they realised no one knew the lyrics to the second verse.

When Kangol began, 'One More Step Along the World I Go,' it was too much for Rob. He stifled a laugh and walked through the walls to see what was going on outside. He was just in time for the arrival of the police.

I Am The Resurrection

Blue and red lights filled the world, bouncing off the damp buildings as every copper in town descended on St Peter's and the burning Citz. Cars screeched to a halt in the middle of the road or mounted the pavement and grassland outside the church. Rob watched as doors crashed open and black-clad bobbies tumbled into the street, hefting riot shields as they raced towards the stricken club. Two fire engines took the corner at speed and weaved through the police vehicles. Everything was chaos, and the zombies moved like a tide as the world filled with noise and fresh meat.

Inside the church, the group heard the commotion and believed their prayers had been answered. Skinhead kicked down his second door of the evening and they raced into the night, piling into the back of the nearest police van. In the chaos and the fear, Rob's zombie was swooped up in their midst, and he sat with a strange smile on his face as the doors slammed shut. The cop was confused and more than a little nervous. He was pretty sure people didn't normally climb into the van of their own accord, but then he caught sight of a burning woman sucking a thumb that wasn't hers and put his foot down. There's duty, and then there's bollock-shrivelling terror. The van sped away, and Rob could do nothing but watch as it careened across the grass, bounced off the kerb, and disappeared down Lord Street, taking his body with it.

"Bollocks!" the dead man swore. This was all getting a bit much. He needed a break. What else could the afterlife possibly throw at him?

As it turns out, a zombie priest.

A scream came from a group of girls heading for a night out. Behind them, appearing from the shadows of the church door, the throatless priest strode forward with his arms wide and his eyes blank.

"Now you're taking the piss," Rob said as the girls ran through him, the dead padre hot on their high heels. He watched them go and wondered if whatever passed for the soul of the young man was now with God like he had believed. He hoped so. It would be horrible to lead your whole life believing in something only to get to the end and find out you had it all wrong. He looked around at the utter chaos—at the falling bodies and the rising corpses. "I am the resurrection," he sang, but then choked on the words as the priest caught a girl by the ponytail. Christians believed in resurrection, didn't they? He remembered that much from school, but as he watched the dead preacher, he was pretty sure this was not what they had in mind. The remaining girls were dragged away by the police, vanishing behind the lines. The cops put up a hell of a fight, but this wasn't the USA; they didn't have guns, and no amount of riot training can prepare you for someone who just won't stay down. Tasers flashed and truncheons beat against heads and bodies, but they were on the back foot. Ambulance crews desperately tried to get people in the back of their vans, but they couldn't be certain which of the injured were liable to take a chunk out of a helping hand. It was the firemen who fared best; they had full protective clothing and helmets, after all. And axes. Big, bloody axes.

People came running from the streets and houses to see what was going on and Rob shrugged and sat down. Nothing draws a crowd like a fight. Society never changes. It's been like this since the tell-tale huddles in the playground, but it's not every day you see a person rise from the dead and try to eat a policeman's face, so most of the onlookers rewrote what they saw to fit their own narrative, which, oddly enough, wasn't too far from the truth.

"Look at them, off their tits, they are!"

"What do you mean?"

"Drugs, innit."

"Bloody smackheads!"

"It's the parents' fault."

"Aye. And the schools."

"The schools?"

"Since they banned the cane. The country's gone soft."

"You're not wrong."

"Look at that bugger, high as a kite. Trying to bite that bobby."

"Definitely stoners."

"Maybe it's that Millennium Bug?"

"That's computers!"

"What is?"

"The Millennium Bug. It's a computer virus."

"You can catch a virus from a computer?! Well, I never!"

"Jesus Christ!" Rob muttered, then added a quick, "sorry," with a guilty glance at the church. It loomed over him with centuries of judgement steeped into its stones, but there were no answers here. Well, he didn't need God. He had something better.

A mam.

'Make a list,' she always said. 'Think it through.' Church seemed as good a place as any to organise his thoughts. He counted on his fingers.

"One, you're dead. That's a bit shit. Two, you're still here... sort of." He shook his head and started again. "One, you're dead. Two, you're a ghost. Three, your body is a zombie. Four, there are now—" he looked around, "—a shit-ton of zombies having a jolly-boy's outing. Five, there aren't any other ghosts. Six, religion appears to be taking a day off. Sorry," he said again, "but, well... prove me wrong?"

He looked up.

He waited.

He nodded.

He sighed.

"Seven, I want to go home. Eight, I can sort of touch things if I try really hard. Nine, the last time I did that I woke up where I died. Ten, *what the bloody hell did he get up to with that barmaid?*"

Deep in thought, Rob watched as another fire engine and a riot van rolled up. It was hard not to be impressed by the bravery on display. One firefighter had lost her helmet, but she screamed orders and the men fell into line beside her. The emergency crews had been reluctant to cause too much harm—they were all trained to do the opposite, after all—but it only takes a few of your mates being ripped apart and eaten for morals and ethics to go down the loo. Under the leadership of the helmetless firefighter, they fought back. The line was quickly bolstered by the newly arrived riot cops and miraculously they began to get the upper hand. They drove forward like Romans behind a shield wall, breaking ranks only to rain down blows on the snarling dead. Zombies were bludgeoned and beaten in a steady rhythm and when the horses arrived, Rob thought they might just win. There's nothing more intimidating to a crowd of rioting footy hooligans than an eight-foot shire horse trained not to flinch, but of course, these weren't footy hooligans. Well, not all of them. One was a granny!

The horses did seal a victory for the living, but not in the way Rob hoped. It was the priest that did it. Still with his arms spread wide, still in some sort of strange supplication to Christ, still living his movie dream, he stepped in front of a charging animal and was smashed from his feet, but somehow, appallingly, his arms wrapped around the horse's neck, and he began to eat.

"Eleven," Rob said. "Not just humans."

The horse and rider fell with a scream and the horde (yes, we're getting there) descended on the stricken animal like a gang of sugar-hyped kids on a burst piñata. The police waded in, blissfully heavy-handed, and before long, remarkably, it was all over. People still screamed, fires still blazed, and terrible, grainy photographs were taken on one or two instant Kodak cameras. But then all eyes turned heavenward as a bright light burst from the sky and lit up a patch of grass outside the church, which, to the living onlookers at least, appeared empty.

For Rob, it was different.

For Rob, it was like the spotlight on *Stars in Their Eyes*, only much more spectacular.

He looked up and shielded his eyes, and for a moment, for just a sweet moment, he believed.

I'm saved!

The light washed over him, and prayers of apology and gratitude made their way to his lips as miraculous and incomprehensible tears spilled down his cheeks. But then, a helicopter landed on his head.

He screamed and had a little tantrum.

The huge rotors of the sleek black machine whipped up smoke and mist as soldiers poured out, armed to the teeth with high-powered rifles. The priest, who had somehow survived the beating from the coppers, rose to his feet once more, his face covered in blood and gore. Rob stepped from the helicopter and barely even blinked as the man's head exploded in a shower of red mist and black sludge. The sound of the gunshot came a split second after, cracking an echo around the houses and church.

"Well, that was kinda cool," Rob said.

The newcomers knew exactly what they were doing. They stalked through the bodies putting bullets into the heads of anyone on the ground. They didn't even bother to check. The gathering crowd protested but thought better of it when a man barked orders and the soldiers turned. It's amazing how quickly an angry mob can disperse when someone with true authority arrives on the scene. Once again, Rob was reminded of the playground. Some teachers got laughed at when they tried to break up fights, but if Mr Evans marched onto the field, all the loud-mouthed boys screaming, "Fight, fight, fight," suddenly found their balls shrivelling and an irresistible urge to be early for double German.

Rob moved closer to the man in charge, keen to hear what he had to say. He was talking to the firefighter, instantly recognising the one person who had taken control.

"Is that the last of them?" he demanded.

"Can't be sure, sir, but I think so."

"What about the building?"

"All dead."

"Staying that way?"

"Sir."

"Good."

"Sir?"

"Yes?"

The woman paused, brushing her hair behind her ear, and tried to find the words. In the end, she settled with, "What the fuck?"

The man looked at her, then handed over a card. She put it in her pocket without looking. This seemed to impress him. "Training exercise," he said.

"Thought so."

"It's over now."

Rob thought of a handsome rock zombie sitting in the back of a packed police van and knew with all the certainty of an impending *Police Academy* sequel that the soldier was wrong. This was far from over.

As if to emphasise his thoughts, the police horse kicked itself upright, exposing a flank licked clean to the rib cage, and bit off a cop's head before anyone could even lift a rifle. There was a moment of awestruck horror and revulsion then gunfire exploded in the night. The dead beast kicked and bucked and finally fell with a meaty thud.

Rob, however, barely registered any of this. His eyes were fixed firmly on a familiar car weaving through the emergency vehicles, following the route the van had taken towards the police station. He'd recognise it anywhere.

A Stratos Silver, 1980 Ford Capri.

His father's car.

Caught by the Fuzz

Rob legged it along Lord Street without the need for adverbs like "breathlessly" or clichés like "his heart raced a mile a minute." He just ran. The thought occurred again that he should be faster. He was a ghost, after all; his muscles didn't ache, and his heart had permanently stopped pounding. So what was stopping him from closing this gap faster than Linford Christie's lunchbox?

The road was quiet and gloomy, but it ran down the back of the high street, where the heavy bass from the pubs and clubs thumped through the stone buildings like the pulse Rob no longer had. He willed himself to go faster, crossing Charlotte Street and then Charles Street—both identical, both like the opening scrawl of that famous Mancunian soap opera; perfectly symmetrical houses lined with cars glistening beneath evenly spaced streetlights. It was beautiful in its own way, but there was no time for that. He had to get to his dad. Rob knew without a doubt his old man would be heading for the police station and he could think of only one reason why. Someone had recognised Rob and called his parents. Five minutes of fame lasts just that little bit longer when you come from a small town. His suspicions were confirmed when he stopped on the corner and saw the car, perfectly parked outside the entrance to the huge red-brick building. Rob had never been to the Police Station before. He never had reason to. But he didn't hesitate when he ran between the two sandstone pillars and through the imposing blue door. The place screamed British Army and he wondered if it had been an HQ back in the day, then realised he didn't care.

The front desk was empty, the reception area abandoned. Rob walked through the walls to find his dad, calling out for him even though he knew it was useless.

"Dad! Where are you? It's me, it's Rob, I'm here!"

He ran through the cell doors like they didn't exist. They were all empty except for the last one, but that definitely wasn't his dad—just a drunk fella pissing in the corner singing 'My Heart Will Go On.'

Probably the safest man in town, Rob thought and kept going. He figured his dad would be in an interview room somewhere and he raced up a flight of stairs, not pausing to consider the existential question of whether or not he could.

Rob heard the commotion as soon as he emerged into a brightly lit corridor—raised voices, shouts, anger, fear. He followed the noise through the halls. This was the part of the station the regular punters didn't usually see—a place for the bobbies themselves: offices, bunkhouses, storerooms, evidence lockers, and finally, a large canteen. That's where he found them: the gang from the church, all with their arms raised, clamouring and shouting, pointing at one of the young bell-ringers, who was backed into a corner. The poor kid lifted his hands in defence and bumped into a stack of stained coffee cups. They fell with a smash. It was chaos. Rob looked around for the police to see why they weren't controlling the mob and realised they were part of it. A heavily moustachioed man with three stripes on his arm raised a truncheon towards the young lad and shouted.

"Tell me it isn't a bite!"

"It isn't. It isn't!" the boy said, tears streaming down his red face. "I fell over, honestly."

"Bullshit!"

"Bravo Two Zero!" Rob said. It was oddly comforting to see people he recognised after the violence of the churchyard. He looked around the group. Yes, these were definitely the same people who had piled into the van. That must mean *he* was here somewhere. He searched the crowd, looking for himself, ignoring the unpleasant feeling as he drifted through people's bodies. The volume rose, the vibe growing more dangerous as each person shivered at his passing.

"You saw what happened to the priest!" a woman screamed. "You saw what happened to the others!" She looked like the kind of lovely old lady to volunteer on the Jesus Bus, offering soup, bread, and a friendly ear to wandering drunks or the homeless, except her face was incandescent with rage and she spat as she screamed. "It's the bites what does it! You all seen it! You all seen it with your own eyes. It's the devil's work. He bites you and you're his."

"Mrs Deacon, no!" the boy pleaded. "I gave you a lift to church!"

"Devil!" she screamed.

"She's not wrong, like!" Bravo Two Zero said, shaking with adrenaline. "It is the bites. We all saw it. And that there is bloody teeth marks!" He pointed to the boy's neck and Rob saw what they were all looking at, a bloody circle on the flesh of his neck, just above the shoulder. The frightened kid turned his collar up like Eric Cantona and tried to hide. The group vibrated towards him with palpable malice, backed up by the righteousness of the faithful and the long arm of the law. The old lady started to pray, though there was nothing Christian about her words, and the cop took a threatening step forward.

"They're fucking zombies," someone said, a young man Rob hadn't noticed before. "No one ever says it in the movies, do they? They never actually say the word, but that's what they are and this ain't a fucking movie and we all know what happens when you get bit by a zombie."

"Yeah!"

The assent echoed around the room and Rob could almost sense the tangible shift from group to mob. They inched closer. The boy backed away, knocking more coffee cups over, adding the sharp clatter of porcelain on porcelain to the rising tension.

"And there's always that one scene ain't there, where someone gets bit and tries to hide it because they don't want to make a scene. They don't want to get caught more like it!"

"No. No. It's not a bite!"

"But they turn, don't they? They turn into one of those bitey buggers and that's when everyone who thinks they're safe as houses—"

"No—"

"Who reckons they're gonna live because they're in a bloody shopping mall or a police station—"

"No!"

"That's when it all goes Pete Tong, and everyone dies!"

"Stop!"

"Well, it ain't fucking happening here, mate."

"Deck 'im, Kev!"

"Mrs Deacon! What would Jesus do?"

"He'd fuck you up, sunshine!"

Rob turned away and tried to block out the sounds of screams, smashing crockery, and entirely misunderstood theology. He was not very successful. He left the canteen and carried on the search for his dad and himself.[10]

---

[10] Freud would have a field day!

Fell On Black Days

Rob found his dad in an office on the first floor. He was sitting opposite a uniformed policeman at a cluttered desk, cross-legged as always, a look of strained impatience on his face. Rob knew that look well. His dad never raised his voice, he never shouted, but he could radiate anger if he needed to. When that thick black moustache began to twitch, you knew to walk away. Rob moved into the room, closer to the man he loved, taking in the shape of his head, the line of his jaw, the ears. He saw the way he played with his wedding ring in that absent-minded way he had. He heard the sigh, the throat-clearing cough that was more habit than necessity. All those little ticks and mannerisms that made him… him. Rob felt the sorrow of loss wash over him, gasping as it ripped through his body as if it were no longer devoid of a central nervous system. His heart hurt—he could feel it, a heavy pain in his chest that sat like a stone, a testament to his mental anguish. It wasn't his dad who was dead, but Rob had still lost him. Mam too. Tears flowed from his eyes, and he began to shake. This wasn't fair. It was supposed to be the living who grieved for the dead. It never occurred to him that it might happen the other way around.

"Where's my son, Frank?" his dad said. It didn't surprise Rob that his father knew the copper. He was one of those blokes who knew everyone.

"I'm right here, Dad," Rob said, moving closer.

"He came in with a load of drunks from over The Citz, John," the policeman said. "There's been a big to-do over there. Not sure of the details myself. Seems some sort of fight broke out."

"My Robbie was in a fight?" John Neville said, leaning forward over the desk. "Is he okay? That's my boy, Frank. He doesn't get into fights, and he certainly doesn't go to The Citz. If he was going to go anywhere, he'd pick a spot that had music. Elgin's or somewhere."

"By all accounts, he *was* the music," Frank said.

"I beg your pardon?"

"He was on stage. He played a few songs."

"I'd hardly call that playing a few songs," Rob said.

"Are you sure?"

"Positive. Everyone knows your boy these days, John. What with him being on TV and whatnot. Here, what was it like? You know, being at a proper studio? You took him, didn't you? What's that Matthew Kelly like?"

Rob's dad didn't answer but the corner of his mouth curled slightly, making the moustache dance. Thankfully, the copper had been in the job a long time and he lifted his hands.

"Sorry. Sorry. Not the time. Look, John. He's in a spot of bother. You see, he wasn't very cooperative when he came in. Wouldn't speak to the desk sergeant at all, and there was a kerfuffle—"

"What are you saying?"

"Dad, it's not me! I'm not there anymore. I'm dead!"

His dad blinked and his eyes flicked towards Rob for just a split second before looking away. Rob gasped as a surge of hope rattled through his ethereal form.

"I'm here, Dad!" he shouted. "I'm here! Can you hear me?"

"What I'm saying, John, is go easy on the lad. Perhaps the fame got to his head a little bit, but he did cross a line."

"Dad!"

"What do you mean?"

"I think he's taken something."

"I didn't, Dad!" Rob spluttered, the instant denial working its way to his lips before he even thought of the irony. "Well, I did, but—"

"For crying out loud, Frank!" John snapped, getting to his feet. "Stop beating around the bloody bush and tell me what happened."

"Fine. But you aren't going to like it. Your boy was at The Citz. As far as we can tell, a fight broke out at closing time and there was a fire. The fight spilled into St Peter's yard. You know the place—"

"Aye, I do. Drove past there on my way here. Saw all the cars and whatnot. Christ almighty, that was a fight?"

Rob could see the change coming over his father, the emotions vying for attention behind the thick moustache. The expression was set and hard, but it was his eyes that gave the game away. He was no longer angry. He was worried.

"We had to send everyone, John. It got a little tasty, but your lad was smart, don't worry. He jumped in the back of the paddy wagon with a group who had been trying to avoid the trouble. Look, some of the details are a little sketchy, the driver's a new lad and honestly, I don't think he's cut out for the job. They don't make them like they used to. Short story is," he added hurriedly as the moustache twitched, "short story is, a group of people who weren't involved in the fight hid in the back of the police van and scared the new lad so bad he drove them all back here. They're all down the hall now, in the canteen with Sergeant Frost, having a cup of tea while we wait for all this to blow over.

"And my boy is with them?"

"No."

"Frank!"

"We had to lock him up, John. He... he bit someone!"

There was a moment of stunned silence in which the moustache didn't move at all. Rob groaned and watched as his father faced off against the copper. The older man shook his head slowly and looked to the ground.

"Not my boy," he whispered.

"No, Dad. It's not. I'm right here." Rob tried to push his dad, but he was too choked up with emotion and his hands passed right through him. The older man shivered.

"Christ alive. Are you sure, Frank? My boy, *my* Robbie—he *bit* someone!"

"I'm sorry, John. It was all a bit hectic. We think someone is pushing a new drug. He's not the only one."

"Drugs?! Where is he? Is he in the cells?"

"No, I put him in the meeting room down the hall and then I called you."

Rob's dad nodded and he calmed himself with a substantial, moustache-trembling effort. "Thank you, Frank," he said, after a minute. "I appreciate that. Take me to him, please."

Rob followed behind the two men with a strange sense of foreboding and guilt. It was like being called to the head teacher's office, that long walk down the school corridor while all other kids sat in their classrooms, the stomach-churning fear of what might happen when you got there, the terror they might call home. Well, that ship had already sailed. Rob walked with his head down and his shoulders hunched as though he might shield himself from whatever came next, but then the realisation hit him that guilt and getting into trouble were not the real problems here. The real problem was the fact his dad was walking towards a fucking zombie!

"Shit!"

Rob raced ahead of the two men, frantically checking rooms and running as fast as he could. He knew, with all the certainty of a cinematic cliché, that it would be the very last room on the corridor, but he couldn't risk missing it. So, he ran half in and half out, sprinting through plasterboard, brick, and steel. All the lights were out up here, and it got darker and darker the further he went. A fire door sat in the end wall with a dim emergency exit sign above, flickering on and off, casting dull green light on the dirty white walls. It all added to the increasingly creepy atmosphere, which Rob thought was entirely unnecessary.

Behind him, his dad stalked through the descending gloom, searching for his son, entirely unprepared for the fact he was about to find a reanimated corpse with a terminal case of the munchies.

Live-In Skin

Rob found his body behind the last door on the left. It stood silently in the corner, staring at the wall. The room was dimly lit by a small desk lamp and there were a few filing cabinets and two chairs. The place had a deeply institutionalised look emphasised by rising damp and a thick layer of dust. It suited a corpse.

The footsteps of the two men echoed down the hall and Rob nearly panicked, searching the room for any hint, any clue, any idea of something to do other than watch as an unsuspecting father got eaten by his son. The door was closed, but he wouldn't be able to hold it shut, what other choice did he have?

Then, like the sudden dazzling light from the helicopter, Rob had an epiphany. The idea entered his head fully formed, a terrifying thought that he might be able to fix this after all. Yet again, it was Patrick Swayze to the rescue, but rather than a creepy cuddle with his wife using Whoopi Goldberg as a conduit, Rob was going to climb back in. He was going to possess himself.

Rob was grasping at straws and there weren't that many he could hold onto. Hope is a strange and desperate thing that makes even the most rational people believe in miracles.

Hope.

What a cunt.

The footsteps grew louder, and Rob shrugged. "In for a penny, in for a pound," he said, and stepped into his body.

The sensation was strange. It was different. It… didn't work.

Rob stood there, sharing the same space as his body but entirely unable to connect with it. There was *something* there—something small and alive—but it wasn't him, and it wasn't human. Whatever remained of the wannabe rock star no longer existed in that body. When he had passed his hands through his dad just moments earlier, there had been a surge of connection, some spark of humanity, some hint of the man behind the moustache, but here there was none of that. The *body* was dead. He shuddered. The *thing* he could sense scratched over him like tiny ants, and he concentrated, trying to understand it. There was a life force, but it wasn't necessarily conscious. It was driven. It kept moving. Feeding. Rob stepped away with a feeling of utter revulsion, just as the door opened and the policeman walked in.

"Robbie," the copper said, "I've brought your dad."

Rob screamed and shouted, trying desperately to draw the attention of his father away from the body as it turned. His father's face was unreadable, the moustache twitched, but not in anger. He moved across the room without saying a word and passed through the spirit of his son. Once more he paused and shook himself before lifting his gaze to the creature he thought was his boy. The zombie regarded the two men with cold, grey eyes. There was blood on its mouth. To Rob's horror, his father pulled a hanky from his pocket and dabbed it on his tongue before reaching out to wipe his son's face.

What happened next happened exactly as you might imagine, complete with a slow-motion, elongated, and ultimately ineffectual, "Noooooo!" from Rob.

A dad wiped the blood from the mouth of his son.

And the son bit his finger off.

Cats in the Cradle

There was a moment of shock punctuated by the sickening snap of bone, and a crunch that was far too close to pork crackling for comfort. Rob's father fell, stumbling against the desk and knocking the lamp over. He crashed into the chair and gripped his hand while the policeman grabbed Rob around the waist, pulling him away. The zombie struggled and thrashed, trying to bite the copper but the man had spent his entire adult life wrestling angry young men who thought they were invincible once they'd had a few Stellas. He knew what he was doing. All this happened in near silence, and it was the silence that shocked Rob most. His dad didn't even cry out. He didn't swear. He was far too shocked to make any noise, and now he just sat in the chair, trying to stem the bleeding from the stump of his finger, unable to process the shock of what had just happened. But Rob knew, and he knew what would happen if he didn't act fast. He raced into the flickering corridor and instantly found what he was looking for: a fire axe mounted to the wall.

Rob smashed his fist into the glass without thinking if he could and it shattered on impact. He snatched the axe and raced back into the room. The fight between the policeman and the zombie was still going and Frank was trying to pin Rob's body against the wall, so he didn't see the floating weapon as it came through the door, but John did. His eyes widened in fear and shock but then they darted to the corner of the room and back, and this time, they locked onto the eyes of Rob.

The ghost of Rob.

The real Rob.

"Son?" the man croaked, his voice catching at the sheer enormity of what he was seeing. John Neville was a smart man, an intuitive man, and though he was in agony, it was nothing compared to the pain that rattled through his soul as the truth of the situation washed over him like fire.

His son was dead.

"I'm sorry, Dad," Rob cried, and from the surprise and sorrow in his father's eyes, he knew he had been heard. But there was no time. The axe wavered in his grip as the strain washed over him. He faltered and stumbled, nearly dropping it, but then gritted his teeth and nodded to his dad's hand. "We need—" he panted, but he couldn't finish. The pain was too great; he could feel himself fading. With a bravery Rob could barely fathom, his dad rolled up his sleeve and put his hand on the desk. He knew. Rob shifted his feet and raised the axe. It nearly broke him. He looked at his father and tried to speak, but the words wouldn't come. He swayed, and his dad raised his other hand as if to steady his boy. Their eyes locked, and the unspoken love between a father and son held the gaze for a long moment. Then his dad smiled and nodded his head.

Rob brought the axe crashing down.

He vanished before it hit home.

When I Come Around

"Fuck you, Bill Murray," Rob swore as he stumbled from the car. There were police there now, surrounding the two blood-splattered vehicles, but he didn't bother hanging around to see what was going on. He raced back towards the town, past the beach park, past Vikki who was now cordoned off inside a tent as nervous officers stood guard. He ran past the bus and yet more police, only these weren't guarding anything; these were fighting the undead. Hand to hand, desperate scuffles all over the road and the roundabout. Rob ran on. A body hung half out of the window in the old folks' home, groaning and thrashing beneath heavy petticoats. He kept going. He had no idea how much time he had lost. The night remained dark, and the mist still shrouded the world, but now it danced in red and blue light. Rob ran down Lord Street and saw the televisions blaring in the front rooms. *So much for all the couch potato warnings,* he thought. Staying in and watching the telly had probably saved a few lives. He ran through Fisherman's Square and past The Citz. The fire was under control now, the bodies, by some miracle, already removed. He swore and kept running. How long had he been out? Where were the rest of the zombies? How many were there? He could hear the heavy bass coming from the high street as he ran, all those people in the club, still dancing, still blissfully unaware of the horrors so close, but he had no time. He had to know if his dad got out. He crossed the lights and kept going, glancing down the terraced streets as he did. They each seemed the same—silent images of peace and urban beauty in a night of pure pandemonium. Well, at least it hadn't spread everywhere, not yet. He forced himself on, crossing the last row of houses before the police station.

Which looked like *Assault on Precinct 13.*

There were bodies at the entrance and on the floor behind the front desk. Shouts and screams echoed through the building and Rob ran up the stairs, where he found three men barricading a narrow corridor with riot shields. There were zombies on the other side, scratching and moaning and heaving. Rob recognised the old lady from the church—Mrs Deacon—and Bravo Two Zero, their gun-metal eyes staring through the reinforced Perspex at the frightened food on the other side. The three men retreated, pushed back down the corridor as the dead clawed and snapped.

"Keep it together," one of them gasped. "We can do it."

"What the hell happened? What's got into them?"

"Fucking zombies!"

"It's not zombies! It's drugs."

"What?"

"After they killed the church kid this fucker gave everyone some wraps. Said it'd take the edge off."

"The edge off what? Life?"

"I dunno but it didn't take long for them to all go fucking mental."

"What about the old bird?" the first man asked, pushing his shield into the face of the snarling woman.

"She got bit but then she just carked it. Heart attack I think."

"So, she died?"

"Yeah."

"And came back?"

"Yeah."

"That's fucking zombies, mate!"

As if to prove his point, the old lady scraped her teeth down the shield. It probably would have been scarier if she hadn't been wearing dentures. They popped right out of her mouth and clattered on the floor with a sound like rolling dice.

Rob raced through the cafeteria and saw the aftermath of the men's conversation for himself. The slumped body of the young lad lay surrounded by broken crockery, and judging by the large knife sticking out of his skull, he wasn't about to get up anytime soon. But that grisly sight wasn't the worst in the room. Rob skirted around three crouched figures as they, for want of a better phrase, shared a meal. The fact that meal was on the 'thrashing for its life' side of raw only added to the overall effect. Rob kept going, stumbling into the opposite corridor and racing along until he got to the end. The fire door was wide open, a dark void beneath the flickering emergency exit sign drawing him on. He turned into the room before it, dreading what he might find.

The first thing he saw was the axe. The lamp must have smashed when his dad fell, but the flicker of the green sign from outside the room glistened on the metal blade and long handle. The weapon stood upright, wedged deep into the desk, rising from a pool of blood like the *Evil Dead* equivalent of Excalibur. Rob moved closer, desperate to see but at the same time not wanting to.

There it was.

His father's hand.

For a godawful moment he half-expected it to crawl away across the desk in search of the rest of the *Addams Family,* but it didn't move. It was dead.

His dad's hand.

And there was no sign of the rest of him.

Rob stood there for a long moment, taking it all in. Those were his *father's* fingers. This was the hand that gripped his own while crossing roads, the one that fed him, wrestled with him, and comforted him. This hand gave him medicine and kept him safe, and now it sat on the desk like a shit paperweight, with one finger missing. And... he looked closer... no wedding ring!

Rob checked again. He was right. The ring was gone. In its place was a white band of skin. He was pretty sure zombies didn't give a shit about jewellery.

The horrible hope surged in Rob, and he tried to remember if his dad's car was still parked where he left it in front of the station, but in all the chaos and the mad dash from the beach, he had no idea. All he saw were the bodies and the billowing smoke from the open door as it sat like the entrance to *Dragon's*

Lair.

He turned in the room just as the exit sign flashed, and that's when he saw the body on the floor. If he still had one, his heart would have stopped. For a split second, he feared the worst—which is saying something, given the circumstances—but it wasn't his dad. It was Frank. Frank was dead. Very dead. And there was considerably less of him than before.

Rob didn't react, he didn't flinch. Instead, he just added it to the (very) long list of shit he would try to process later. But he was in a police station, so perhaps it was time to act like a cop. He'd seen *The Bill* enough times.

"Think, dickhead! Think!"

Rob paced back and forth and made a list, ticking off the points like Inspector Poirot relaying his findings. "Dad's alive," he said. "He has to be. And conscious enough to take his wedding ring." He looked at the axe. "But he didn't take the axe, and his friend is dead. So, he either couldn't move it, or he couldn't bring himself to use it… on me." He moved closer to the desk and looked at the long handle of the weapon. There were blood marks on the wood. Fingerprints. One more point. "He tried to take it, but he couldn't get it out. Must've been hard with one hand. So, what then? He wouldn't have just watched his son eat his friend. No, but he's losing blood. He has no hand. And he just saw the ghost of his dead kid chop it off. Chances are, he's probably not thinking straight. So, where is he? And where am I for that matter?"

Rob looked to the floor and saw the bloodstains on the carpet. They led out of the door in a butter-icing drizzle of drops and spills. He followed, leaving the police station by the fire exit and making his way down the steps. Blood pooled on the pavement at the bottom and he followed the drips around the side of the building, onto the main road, where it suddenly stopped in a horribly large puddle. A tyre mark ran through one edge and vanished in fading rubber prints up the tarmac.

"Car," Rob said to himself. "Or an ambulance, maybe? Dad got away. But where—?" His question was cut short by an explosion of gunfire that cracked from the walls and bounced around the streets. He ran towards the sound, racing to the front of the station just in time to see two black-clad soldiers heading for the front door. They passed his father's abandoned car, their rifles raised and flashing in the misty night as they moved inside. The men vanished, and suddenly the street was empty. Gunfire exploded from the building. There were screams. And then, silence.

Rob stood in the middle of the street as a car powered through his body and suddenly it all became too much—the madness, the horror, the grief. It overwhelmed him, and he screamed at the night. Rob was a good singer; it was a good scream. Chris Cornell would've been proud. But this wasn't music. This was anguish.

"What the fuck is going on?!" he roared. "Am I being punished? Is this purgatory? What the fuck did I do to deserve this? Did I eat the wrong meat on the wrong fucking day? Is it because I was about to have sex before marriage? That's a pretty shit rule, man! What the fuck? Where are you?!"

There was no ominous roll of thunder or crash of lightning at his words and Rob knew with a certainty that made his soul ache that he was shouting into the void.

"Fuck you!" he cried. "Fuck you and fuck all the angels and fuck that cat!" he added, as a sleek feline ran across the street. The cat stopped, hissed at him, then vanished into an alley. Rob gave it the finger before sinking to his knees and sobbing into his hands.

He was dead. Vikki was dead. His body nearly ate his dad. This was not the night out he had in mind.

"I want my mam," he said. He pictured her somewhere—perhaps in The Stead hospital—meeting her horrifically injured husband and being given the news about their son. He imagined the pain on her face, and the sadness rose within him, threatening to spill over. But then an explosion rocked the inside of the police station, and screams rattled through the streets from somewhere deep in the terraced houses. Rob barely flinched but suddenly felt ashamed of his selfishness. He wasn't exactly the only one having a difficult night.

"I'm sorry," he sobbed to no one in particular, though he still shook with barely suppressed rage. The anger fed the guilt, and the guilt made the anger grow.

With an effort, Robbie Neville gathered his thoughts. He hummed songs to himself and concentrated, he wasn't entirely sure what he was concentrating on, but his mam's words came back to him. "Just take ten deep breaths, love. It'll be alright after ten deep breaths."

He was dead. He didn't need to breathe, but he did it anyway.

Rob counted them down and smiled to himself as he felt the emotions settle. His mam was right. But then, mams always are, aren't they.

Then suddenly, Rob felt something else, something real. Soft fur pushed against his hands.

The cat was there, brushing against him in that way cats do. Rob scratched it behind the ears without really thinking, and it purred. Then, because it's a cat, it lifted its tail, flashed the Eye of Sauron, and walked away.

It was only after it vanished into the shadows further down Lord Street that Rob realised what had just happened. The memory of the warm touch lingered on his fingers as he looked up in disbelief.

"Holy shit!"

Nancy Boy

Rob followed the cat into an alley, and yet another scene of violence. Though this one had nothing to do with zombies—it was just the usual, disappointing weekend thuggery caused by too many Smirnoff Blacks and too few brain cells. A group of drunk lads in distinctive Burberry caps and scarves were shouting and swearing at a woman in a bright red dress. As Rob moved closer, he realised it wasn't a woman after all, but a tall, muscular man with long blonde hair and immaculate make-up. Suddenly, Rob knew exactly where they were.

This was one of those strange alleys in Redcar that everyone knew, one way or another, though usually for very different reasons. It connected the High Street to Lord Street and was lined with small shops only your granny cares about, full of wool and dress patterns. The stall on the corner, however, was familiar to all the kids in town, stacked with plastic bags of cola bottles, blackjacks, flying saucers, pink chocolate mice, and, of course, candy cigarettes. But it was the building above that drew the night crowd.

In the dank, dirty alley, up a black-painted fire escape, stood the strip club.

The man in the red dress retreated up the steps, clutching a small handbag to his rather ample chest. Rob was confused. He made a very attractive woman, and all the bits seemed to be in the right place. He even spoke in a feminine voice as he raised his hands.

"Please, just leave me alone. I don't want any trouble. Help me, someone."

"There's no one here except us, you fucking tranny!"

The lads egged each other on with the usual brain-dead taunts.

"Go on, Matty. Av 'im! Fucking poofter!"

One of the lads spat over the shoulder of another, and Rob swore at him. He hated spitting. He had been spat on before—it was worse than being punched.

"Oy! You fucking Neanderthal! Piss off!"

The lads didn't hear Rob, of course, but the man in the red dress did. The blonde turned and locked eyes with him. Rob couldn't believe it. First his dad, then the cat, and now…

"You can see me!" he said, desperation and pain clear in his voice. The man's eyes were sad and kind. He nodded.

"I see you, love."

The lads laughed at this.

"Fucking nancy boy is tripping balls, Matty! Kick his head in!"

Another glob of spit landed on the red dress, and the blonde man sighed. He pulled a lace hanky from his bag and wiped the mess with deliberate care. When he looked up, his eyes were hard and dangerous. All tenderness was gone.

"Just a minute, pet," he said to Rob, then he turned to the lads. The change was instant. He walked down the iron steps and the fuckheads in the alley formed a small circle around him. When he spoke again, he did so in a deep, masculine, and above all, angry voice. It was a voice laden with threat and danger but none of the idiots were in any state to appreciate the warning signs.

"This is my favourite dress," he said slowly. "And you ought to treat a lady with more respect." He lifted the bag over his shoulder and stepped forward.

"You ain't no fucking lady!"

"Not right now I'm not," he said.

The beautiful man in the red dress proceeded to give the three lads what can only be described as an absolute hiding. It didn't take long and not once did he drop his bag. He threw punches like a boxer—they never missed, and the sound they made as they connected in that dark alley was like the slap of a butcher's hammer. He moved effortlessly, and Rob was more than a little impressed at the dancing shuffle of his feet. Move like a butterfly, sting like a bee—in high heels. The man's calves glistened as he moved. He had exceptional legs. The three lads got a close-up view as they all hit the deck in quick succession.

When it was over, the man brushed his hair back and spoke again, his voice soft and gentle.

"Now, lovely boys," he purred, "you've had your fun, and I've had my exercise. May I suggest you kindly… fuck off!"

The three lads scrambled to their feet and scarpered—two one way and one the other—not even bothering to stop at the regulation twenty metres to hurl insults.

Rob and the tall blonde were left alone in the silence of the alley. The cat appeared, and the man smoothed down his dress, knelt, and gently scratched the little creature behind the ear. The sound of purring filled the gloom.

"Are you okay?" Rob asked.

"Sweet boy," the man said. "I'm always okay, but what about you? You're a bit… translucent."

"I get tired," Rob said. It was the best he could come up with, and the fact he was having an actual conversation with a living, breathing human wasn't helping his mental acuity.

"Be careful, sweetie. You might vanish."

"That's happened a few times already."

"I didn't mean… never mind. Let's start over. What's your name?"

"I'm Rob."

"Pleased to meet you, Rob. I'm Pauline."

The man called Pauline stood and stretched. He looked Rob up and down with sad eyes. "You look young," he said.

"I'm seventeen."

"Oh, that's no age. Poor lamb, but I meant—" he waved his hand at Rob as if to indicate his body. His nails were just as beautiful as his dress. "You know… a young ghost. How long have you been dead?"

"What time is it?"

The man gasped and held his hands to his lips in shock. "Oh, my Christ! You're just a bairn. Come with me, love. I'll take care of you. But I think we need a stiff drink."

"How—?" Rob began but he couldn't find a suitable end to the question, so he just settled for repeating the start. "How?"

"Don't you worry. I'll explain what I can. Come on now. We'll go in the club and find a dark corner. I know your poor mam probably told you to be careful of strange women, but you can trust your Aunty Pauline."

Lola

Rob followed Pauline into the strip club, marveling at the man as he strode through the tables and chairs. He walked as if he owned the place, as if he belonged. He said hello to everyone he met, blew a kiss at the barmaid, and cat-called a woman on a small stage who grinned and thrust her naked backside in his direction. Pauline playfully pinched the girl on the bottom while she clung to a shining pole, and the man walked away laughing. Rob followed, completely baffled and with no idea where to look. He no longer had the blood flow necessary for many of the urges he might have felt in such a place, but that didn't mean his brain had broken any of the associations. The large room was dark, but with four spot-lit dancers wearing a whole lot of not a lot, it was hard not to stare. Rob swallowed. Arousal without the necessary equipment is quite a complicated process, but the mind is a powerful thing, and Rob's mind was working overtime. He put his head down and followed Pauline through the bar to a dark corner where the man ordered two large whiskeys from a waitress wearing about as much clothing as the lady on the stage. Pauline kissed the woman on both cheeks and waited for his drink while humming The Kink's song, 'Lola.'

"That doesn't fit the mix tape," Rob said. Pauline stopped and looked at him. Rob blinked, not realising he'd said it out loud. "It's erm, I mean, well, I love music. I love The Kinks. They're one of my mam's favourite bands. But it's kind of been all nineties for me tonight."

Pauline smiled as his drinks arrived. "It's not just the music of your own generation that defines who you are," he said in a purring feminine voice.

The waitress clearly thought he was talking to her and smiled. "Too right, sweetie. I was born twenty years too late. Give me the sixties any day." She placed the drinks on the table. "It's not like you to sit by yourself, Pauline. Are you okay?"

"I'm fine, love. Just fancied a spot of quiet."

"Right you are. Give me a wave if you need anything."

"Thank you, darling."

The lady left Rob and Pauline in the dark corner on their own. It was strange to be inside, away from the chaos of the streets, though the thought of his injured dad and meandering body made it hard for Rob to relax. He felt caught on the threshold between two worlds—the vibrant life of the High Street and the absolute chaos of the walking dead. Pauline poured the two glasses together and took a small sip. He giggled as he drank and then looked at Rob.

"I expect you have questions."

"Lots."

"Go on then, young man."

"Are you really called Pauline?"

"Ha ha! Oh, darling, that's not what I was expecting, but I guess this is all a bit new to you."

Rob didn't know if he meant the strip club, being dead, or his companion in the red dress. He wasn't even sure what pronouns to use never mind where to start with the questions, but he needn't have worried. Pauline was the talkative type.

"Outside here, I'm called Ian. I work at British Steel just like everyone else. In the blast furnace."

"Tough job," Rob said. He'd heard his dad say that once and it seemed appropriate. He fidgeted in his seat.

"My turn. How did you die?"

"I'm not sure. Drugs, I think."

"Ah."

"I was with a friend and I… woke up like this."

"And your friend?"

"Dead."

"Drugs?"

"I'm not sure."

"What do you mean?"

"It's hard to explain. My… body. Well, it's like I'm two different people. I'm not sure I *can* explain, to be honest."

"Honey," Pauline said, "you're talking to a man in a bright red dress with fabulous fake tits and killer heels. There's not a whole lot I don't know about two different bodies. Why don't you try me?"

"Well, my body is a zombie."

Pauline coughed and choked on his drink. He fanned himself with his painted nails and tried to get it under control. It took some time.

"Okay, sweetheart. That's a new one. You got me there."

"How is this possible?" Rob asked, leaning forward. "I mean, this—us talking? How can you see me? Hear me?"

"It's a gift, sweetie."

Rob fell quiet, and Pauline waved the waitress over to order a glass of water. When it arrived, he took a long sip and then pulled out a silver case, selecting a clean white cigarette and placing it between his painted lips. Pauline was remarkably relaxed—effortlessly cool. "Normally, I smoke outside," he said. "But I don't suppose you'll mind."

"No, of course not. So, um, have you always been able to talk to dead people?"

"No, sweetheart. Not always." Pauline took a drag from the cigarette and leaned back, closing his long lashes as he exhaled the smoke in a slow plume. "It's hard for people like me, honey," he said. "This is who I am, you see. On the inside. Oh sure, I'm a big, tough burly steelworker by day, but that's not the real me. It's hard to be yourself in this life. I wasn't sure I could ever be. So, a few years ago, I… tried not to."

"I'm not sure I follow."

"I drank the witch's brew, sweetie."

Rob looked at him with a blank face.

"Ten parts vodka, ten parts sleeping pills."

"Oh."

"Bingo."

"Well, I'm glad it didn't work. It's a pleasure to meet you, Pauline."

Pauline smiled and looked away. It was a strangely shy gesture. A hint of moisture clung to his eyes. "Charming boy," he said. "You're going to make me cry."

"I'm sorry. I—" Rob was floundering. He had never been in a strip club before. He had never spoken to anyone like Pauline before. He… well… he'd never been dead before. This wasn't how he pictured it at all. It seemed particularly surreal to be having a good old natter in the middle of a zombie outbreak. Rob hung his head. Fat lot of use he was anyway. All he did was run around and poke things. He looked at the cigarette in Pauline's fingers and tried to gather his thoughts.

"So… after that, you could see dead people and started dressing—" Rob trailed off, unsure how to finish his thought, but he needn't have worried; Pauline burst out laughing.

"Oh, sweetie, no. Not this, anyway," he said, framing his face in a Madonna-style vogue. "Been dressing like this since I was a wee boy. You should've seen the first time my old man caught me. Whoa, Nelly! Did I get in trouble!"

"I'm so confused."

"Sweetie, I've always been what the charming boys outside refer to as a tranny. It's who I am, and I make no excuses for it. I'm fucking fabulous!"

"Yes, you are," Rob grinned, understanding immediately where he was going wrong with his pronouns. He smiled at Pauline. *She* was, indeed, fucking fabulous. "So, the ability to talk to dead people came later?"

"Exactly. It's not the answer I was looking for, but it has certainly made things interesting. You're the first ghost I've seen in a few weeks, though. It's been quiet."

"There are others?"

"Of course, sweetie."

"Oh, thank… God."

Pauline laughed at the pause. Rob was warming to her by the second. She got him. She was easy to talk to. Shyness, it seemed, was the preserve of the living.

"It's only been a few hours, but it's been so hectic and… lonely. You have no idea what is going on out there."

"Never mind that for now. You're not lonely anymore, love. Aunty Pauline is here. Tell me everything."

So, Rob did. What else could he do? He had no idea where his body was, or where his dad was, and every time he touched something, he faded away until he woke up back in the car park. Rob had gone the way of the Dodo, and the only person he could talk to was Pauline. She was his Charon, halfway between the living and the dead. He had cried out for guidance, and instead of an angel or a ferryman on the River Styx, he discovered a strapping six-footer in a beautiful red dress somewhere between the High Street and Lord Street. Life, and death, it seemed, was not without a sense of style.

Tonight, Tonight

Rob begged Pauline to go straight home. He had no doubt she could handle herself but there's a big difference between fighting off a group of bigoted chavs and surviving a zombie apocalypse. The last thing he wanted was an undead Aunty Pauline getting bloodstains on her bright red dress.

In the end, they came up with a plan, and Rob walked Pauline home. Her flat was just off the High Street, which was remarkably peaceful considering the chaos in the backstreets. Heavy bass from the clubs thumped through the air but receded into the background when they ducked down an alley towards the seafront and Pauline's flat.

"You're a real gentleman," Pauline said, lifting her hand to Rob's cheek and holding it close. Rob was desperate for the contact, but this wasn't the time to waste whatever little energy he had. That's what it boiled down to, Pauline surmised—energy, effort, and timing.

All ghosts have some telekinetic power, she told him, but it came at a cost. It's the reason spirits famously haunt the same place or repeat the same actions over and over; it's why Rob had returned twice to the place he died. There were ties. The ghosts she knew—those who haunted Kirkleatham Museum, Locke Park boating lake, and the fish and chip shop in Dormanstown—all stayed pretty much where they were. Rob was different. Rob was unusual. He seemed to have the run of the town—until he ran out of energy and disappeared—and that, Pauline said, was scary. She only knew of one type of ghost that became completely invisible in the spiritual plane.

Poltergeists.

"And they're all bastards," she'd said. "They sacrifice physical form for power, but once you've lost your body, you lose sight of who you are, of the things that make you... *you*. That's why they're all evil buggers dragging little kiddies through television sets and whatnot. They don't know any better. The more you change, the less of yourself you feel. The less you feel, the more you change."

Their conversation had been long and fascinating, but unfortunately, it couldn't go on forever. The night wore on, and as it did, the dead continued to roam the streets of the small seaside town. It was when Pauline told Rob of her favourite ghost ("apart from you, sweetie") that the seeds of their plan were formed, and Rob now knew what he was going to do with the rest of his night.

Part two, if you will.

Pauline's (second) favourite ghost was an old man in a flat cap who waited near the town's famous clock tower for the last double-decker to New Marske. He was a charmer, heading to meet his wife, always carrying daisies, always dressed sharp, always excited. But each evening, as the bus groaned its way along Coast Road, the old man vanished, reappearing back in town where he was forced to wait until the next night, destined to repeat the same journey over and over. Pauline spent hours with him, chatting on the bench near the butchers as he waited. She spoke to all the spirits she met if they let her. She loved their stories and understood their loneliness. She couldn't be sure, she explained, but in her heart, she believed those who got left behind had some sort of purpose to fulfil, something they needed to do. It seemed like an awful cliché, but clichés are all born somewhere. The old man needed to get to his wife. Perhaps then he would move on to whatever comes next?

"I like that," Pauline had said in a low voice as they left the club. "It gives life meaning. It gives us a sense of destiny. It can all change. You're not stuck."

For Rob, it seemed clear. He had to stop his body from getting into any more mischief.[11] At the very least, they agreed, it was the right thing to do.

* * *

"Are you going to be alright?" Pauline asked, after unlocking the door and switching on a lamp just inside her apartment. Rob blinked in the sudden light, shaking himself out of his reverie and nodding.

"Yeah. I'll be okay."

He tried not to stare. It was the first time he had seen Pauline in full light, and she made a striking figure. She was older than he first thought, with crow's feet and a strong jaw, though the make-up was still perfect. Rob could see the man beneath the woman and the lady beneath them both. Behind her, the house was full to the brim with bright colours and beautiful green plants—warm and inviting.

"Are you sure?" Pauline asked.

"I'm dead, Pauline. What else can happen to me?"

"You know what I mean."

"I do. Thank you."

"So, tell me your plan again."

"I'm going to find my body and push it into the sea," Rob said. It annoyed the hell out of him that this was the best bet. He had been so close just a few hours ago. The guilt ate at him.

"You know it would be easier for me to do it."

"No," he said. He didn't need the added guilt of putting Pauline in danger. "We discussed this. One slip, one bite, and it's game over."

"But you might vanish once you're done. You won't be able to visit anyone."

"I saw my dad," Rob said, his voice small and strained. Pauline made a noise in her throat and stepped outside, gathering Rob in her arms in a hug he wished he could feel.

Rob felt a single large sob rattle his chest as Pauline's arms wrapped around

---

[11] Which is a lovely 'Pauline' way of saying to stop him from eating people and turning them into walking corpses.

him, then he pulled away. "Just in case," he said with smoky tears in his eyes.

"Just in case," Pauline echoed. "Be safe, Robert Neville. I'll lock this up tight against any marauders, but you feel free to drift through my door anytime if it doesn't work out."

"Thank you. And remember—"

"Call the police, I know, pet. But considering what you told me about the old station, I think they already know."

"Not if they're all dead."

"Then the army lads will take care of it. You'll see. They'll be calling them in from Catterick, and by morning this town will be full of squaddies. Something to look forward to," she added with a wink. "It'll be just like *Soldier Soldier*. I do like that Jerome Flynn, but don't worry," she said as he started to protest, "I'll still call. You just concentrate on finding that body of yours."

A scream shattered the night, rattling through the alley and bouncing from the walls. Rob saw Pauline flinch. She may have been hard as nails, but the threat of being eaten alive was a great leveller. They smiled at each other, and Pauline vanished behind the closed door with a blown kiss. There was another scream. Rob waited for the click of the lock and the deadbolts to slide into place before racing towards the noise, which, somewhat anticlimactically, turned out to be a group of drunk girls heading out for a dance.

Celebrity Skin

The fact the world still turned pissed Rob off. He knew it was selfish, but as he followed the giggling gang of short skirts and long jackets, he couldn't help but feel a bit miffed that the universe didn't seem to give a rat's arse he was dead. There was no 'Stop all the clocks, cut off the telephone,' it was business as usual, on earth as it is in heaven.

"Fucking heaven!" he swore. Well, if he found his body and somehow put an end to this, maybe he'd find out?

There was a connection, Pauline had said, between the ghosts and something that tied them to this world. For him, it was probably the violence of his death and the bizarre situation that allowed his body to come back, but that just raised more questions. He'd seen more than his fair share of people die this evening, and not one of them had stuck around to shoot the shit. Sure, the bodies got up and wandered off, but what happened to the rest? Where was the soul? The ghost? The spirit? The damn bedsheet with eyeholes cut out?

There were so many unanswered questions, and a very small part of Rob wondered if he'd just passed out in the backseat of Vikki's car, and this was all a drug-induced hallucination.

Nah, that would be terrible. Not the waking up part, but the godawful lazy storytelling. At the very least, he hoped the universe had a better writer.

* * *

It is probably worth another pause here to ponder two important things, the nature of stories and the nature of Redcar town itself. Sometimes, bizarre events occur simply to move the plot along. New characters—or even old ones—appear as if from nowhere to drive the story on and keep the world turning. We call this *Deus ex Machina,* or 'God from the machine.' The only problem here is people decry sloppy coincidences, but they're missing the point. Coincidence is what life is all about. Where would we be without it?

It is, for example, entirely coincidental that a new batch of drugs found its way to a small seaside town in the northeast of England when they could have quite easily gone to any major city: London, Manchester, New York, or San Francisco. The Venga Bus could have taken them anywhere. But it didn't; it took them here—a small town with a distinctive High Street. The type of place where all kinds of hell can break loose among the terraced houses in the back streets, but just a stone's throw away, the nightclubs still bounce with happy punters utterly oblivious to the carnage. And it's those punters—four young women in short skirts, giggling and laughing and making their way to Club Kudos—that are going to drive this story forward. Not that they know it... yet. 'Stop all the clocks, cut off the telephone.' Not here, love. There's still two hours of dancing to be had.

And in a twist of fate, or an alignment of the stars, or because the town is so small there really is nowhere else to go, there just so happened to be a handsome dead guy standing between the girls and the club.

Where he came from and how he got there, Rob had no idea, but his body stood nonchalantly near the hobby shop as though it didn't have a care in the world. *Nice to see you, to see you... nice!* The building itself was an anomaly in the higgledy-piggledy mass of stores and pubs, a throwback to a bygone age of tall townhouses with triangle rooftops and doors in the middle. Rob's body was doing something it had done a million times before, staring through the window at the toy trains and cars on the other side of the glass. It made no sense that he was there, but then, none of this made sense, and Rob didn't have time to question things because the girls were racing across the road towards... him.

"Rob! Hey, it's Rob from TV!"

"Give over!"

"It is. We were in Science together."

"The lad who did Kurt Cobain?"

"Yeah! He's a celebrity!"

"Hey, Rob!"

"Christ," the real Rob muttered, and jogged after the group. The girl in the lead had indeed shared a science class with him but that was about all they'd shared. He was surprised she even knew his name. She was one of those girls in school who existed in entirely different circles and never so much as looked outside her own[12] but herein lies the nature of small towns all over the globe, five minutes of fame can change everything.

The girl, Leanne something, Rob couldn't remember, draped herself over his body and he flinched in anticipation, but nothing happened. There was no bite, no snarl, no reaching arms. Just the dazzling eyes and perfect hair. And blood. There was blood all over the young man's mouth, though remarkably little on his shirt.

"Oh my god!" Leanne cried. "Have you been in a fight?" There was something in her voice Rob didn't like. It wasn't shock. She was thrilled. "That's so rock and roll! What are you up to? Come to Kudos with us. Go on. I work there but it's my night off. I'll get you in for free—" she paused and bit her lip, "as long as you dance with me. I always had a crush on you, you know."

"Jesus Christ!" Rob said. In this instance, he was pretty sure God wouldn't mind a little repetitious blasphemy.

Leanne wrapped her arm through Rob's and steered him along, the other girls giggling and laughing, taking a backseat to her leadership. Rob could only guess what his body had been up to since he last saw it, but he was also pretty sure it would be a guess damn close to the mark, which probably meant

---

[12] This was the late '90s in England. It wasn't like the movies you see of American schools. There were no uniformed collections of Jocks, Nerds, and Cheerleaders. About the closest England had back then were the Hard lads, the Fit girls, and a slowly emerging group of Goths and Indie kids. It would be a few more years before anyone even heard the word 'Emo.' For now, it was just one letter short of everyone's favourite Muppet.

there was another body somewhere close. As the group crossed the end of Redcar Lane, Rob looked towards St Peter's Church and saw it: the stumbling figure doing the recognisable fox-trot shuffle of the walking dead, banging against the window of the God shop. A light flickered inside, holding its attention, and even from this distance, he could see the gaping wounds in the arms and shoulders, the flesh missing from the neck and face. Rob looked around. It was so surreal. The high street was relatively quiet but the world behind it was in chaos. All the girls had to do was turn their heads to the right. The lights of the emergency vehicles bounced off the buildings down near the church, but no one took a blind bit of notice. They were pulled towards the pulse of the club like blood to a heart. Rob stopped in the street and watched as a mushroom cloud of black smoke rose over the terraced houses, somewhere near the allotments. When he turned back, the gang was at the entrance to the club, a giggling, laughing mess of fawning arms and being cool by association.

"Do you know who this is?" he heard Leanne declare, and the group vanished inside, a bouncer calling up the stairs to get the lad cleaned up first.

Underage, covered in blood, wearing ripped jeans, a black t-shirt, and a pair of knackered Converse—oh, and you know, *being dead*—and he *still* got into the nightclub! Rob couldn't believe what he was seeing. Celebrity skin will get you everywhere, he thought. Unfortunately, the bigger thought—that his zombie had just been invited into a packed club while he did sod all to stop it—hit him like a half-brick in a sock.

"Bollocks, Rob!" he cursed himself. "You had one job!"

Rockafeller Skank

Rob had never been in Kudos before. In fact, he'd never been in a nightclub before, so all his expectations were based on music videos and TV shows. As he walked up the dark stairs to the top floor, he had half an idea it might look like the set of *TFI Friday*. It didn't.

He reached the cloakroom desk just as Leanne reappeared from the back with a pristine zombie in tow. She held his hand and strode through the thronged masses, demanding they move. And they did. People stared and pointed, nudging their friends. Word spread like a virus, and the crowd parted, making way as the local celebrity was led straight to the dance floor.

There were shouts, cheers, and heckles, but the music was so loud it all blended into a bass-filled roar. The seas that opened to let the zombie and Leanne through closed behind them, a mass of grinding, shifting bodies. Lights flashed, people laughed, girls screamed, and all the while, the dead body of a wannabe rock star was gyrated against like a pole in a strip club.

The ghost of Rob, the real Rob, once again couldn't quite believe what he was seeing. His dead body was enjoying the afterlife far more than he was. Hell, it was enjoying life far more than he ever had!

Rob stood on the dance floor like a strange voyeur, apologising every time someone danced through him.

"Sorry. Excuse me. Pardon me. My fault."

Maybe this *was* hell—a particularly British kind of hell.

The music changed, and the tempo shifted—heavier, faster. Arms were raised in the air, and bodies pushed against each other in a claustrophobic nightmare, and Rob still stood like a numpty. It wasn't his scene anyway. He hated this stuff. Leanne, unsurprisingly, was all in: arms above her head, boobs in Rob's face, and her bare midriff shining in the blinking lights as hundreds of voices joined in the world's easiest lyrics—and still got them wrong.[13]

"Right about then!"

Nightclubs are utterly bizarre places when a person is sober.

"The small punk mother!"

All those people screaming and singing, crammed in like sardines.

"Check him out then!"

Trapped in small worlds among the masses.

"The small punk mother!"

Only those who work behind the bar truly know what it's like.

"Right about then!"

And the unspeakable nonsense people think they can get away with in the anonymity of a crowd.

"The small punk mother!"

Rob was seeing all this for the first time, detached, passive, staggeringly inexperienced. He just didn't know where to look.

"Check it out then!"

Leanne's arms were high in the air, her eyes fixed on Rob, her body pulsing with the beat.

"The small punk mother!"

The zombie lifted his hands to her bare stomach.

"Right about then!"

Leanne placed something in her mouth and bit her lip.

"About then!"

Rob's hands caressed her belly.

"About then!"

It was almost tender.

The bass dropped. Everybody screamed. And Rob's zombie thrust his

---

[13] Not in any small part due to copyright reasons.

thumbs into Leanne's belly button and tore her stomach wide open.

Ebeneezer Goode

As it turns out, ghosts *can* vomit. Rob wasn't quite sure *what* he just threw up because he was on the upper floor of the nightclub, and whatever ethereal sputum left his mouth vanished through the dance floor. By the time he looked back up, the scene before him had... barely changed. People still danced, the music still played, and Leanne was still alive. Not for very much longer, mind you, but the poor girl was hanging on. Literally. Rob's zombie had her entrails in his mouth, and Leanne had the other end in her hands. Her face was white, her mouth forming an 'o' of a silent scream, but then it closed. She tugged, shuddered, cried, and *then* she died—still on her feet, still crammed in on all sides. While Rob's zombie ate.

It took a bizarrely long time for anyone to notice, but when the first dancer slipped on the rapidly growing pool of blood and crashed to the floor, dragging others down with her, it all began to unravel. Rob watched as the circle widened and people screamed, running for the exits. Bizarrely, though, it didn't spread too far. It couldn't. The club was rammed. Most people were still dancing, and when the Fatboy Slim track eased seamlessly into the familiar synth of 'Ebeneezer Goode,' more rushed in to join the mass of dancers. The gaps closed, and the whole club sang out the only words they could all agree on. Arms were raised and eyes closed. Screams rang and people ran, but the majority didn't notice. By the time the song hit the first chorus, it was as if nothing had happened.

But it had.

Rob's zombie stopped eating and stared at Leanne with uncomprehending eyes. She looked back at him; perfectly unaware the short crop top now showed far more of her belly than was entirely healthy. Her eyes glimmered like polished steel. Together, the two zombies moved in the push of the jostling crowd.

It was kind of cute in a really fucked up sort of way.

A Prat[14] of Tommy Hilfiger-clad lads bounded onto the dance floor, so caught up with the music they didn't see anything amiss as they threw obligatory white-rapper shapes like they were drowning. One of them hit Leanne with an elbow to the head and she turned.

Here we go, Rob thought.

To the lad's credit, he did try to apologise, but something about the proximity of those dazzling grey eyes stopped him in his tracks while the thrust of her boobs hid most of the damage. That, coupled with the fact he'd only just worked out the lyrics to the song were *"E's are good,"* which he found hilarious considering the small baggy he had in his jeans, all led to a perfect storm of ignorance, happiness, and a momentary pause that would, ultimately, end his life. Tommy Hilfiger blinked, tried to comprehend everything in the space of a few seconds, got instantly horny when the cute girl leaned into his neck, and then died remarkably quickly when she ripped out his throat.

* * *

As Dr Ian Malcolm said, life finds a way. So, it seems, does death. The virus inside the reanimated bodies had the exact same desire and primal urge as most of the patrons in the club. It wanted to move, and it wanted to find something warm to play with. Who can blame it? The ghost of Rob watched in horror as it spread through the masses. Small scuffles broke out, and the bouncers came running, but that was nothing new; it was Saturday night. 'Ebeneezer Goode' changed into Robert Miles's 'Children,' and those completely lost in the music closed their eyes and raised their hands to the sweat-soaked ceiling. They never stood a chance. It rippled through the

[14] Collective noun.

crowd like a shit version of the 'Macarena,' only instead of a unified shindig that looked a bit like *The Three Amigos*' salute, people were being fucking eviscerated by gnashing teeth and searching fingers! A good firm grip will tear most flesh if you're hungry enough.

The scuffles turned into fights, and people crashed into one another in their haste to escape. Skin was ripped from faces and devoured, feet slipped on pools of slick blood and God knows what else, but amongst it all, miraculous pockets of dancers kept going—small islands of pissed-up ravers in a sea of death. There were screams all around the nightclub now; they grew louder and more intense, and suddenly the dam burst. Eyes opened, heads turned, people died, and the rest ran. The music still played, but the DJ was dead, already reanimated and trying to eat a tall spotty lad with glasses who beat him away with a bottle of lemon Hooch. Rob's body was lost in the chaos, buffeted back and forth by the terrified crowd and the roaming undead. One of the bouncers tried to halt the tide, but he vanished beneath trampling feet as people surged down the stairs. Doors into back rooms flung open as people dove over bars to escape. The staff were already gone, abandoning their minimum-wage posts for the hope of safety, or at the very least, a head start.

Then the lights came on.

The screams hit a whole new level as the true horrors were revealed, which, to be fair, is fairly common when the lights go up in a club, but there usually wasn't this much blood. Amidst the chaos, Rob caught sight of his body heading backwards at a fair lick. It was trapped in a crowd, hemmed in on all sides as it was carried along in a scrum, then pushed through a door to the club downstairs.

Because Kudos was a two-parter. Happy hardcore, chart-topping dance music here on the top floor and below—well, below was another world. A world of heavy guitars, black nail polish, and charity shop army jackets.

Below them was The Piper.

Smells Like Teen Spirit

'Smells like Teen Spirit,' was playing when Rob burst through the terrified blockade on the stairs and into the room below. It was a wall of noise. His second-favourite Nirvana song pulsed through every inch of space at ear-splitting volume. *This* was the tune he really wanted to play on *Stars in Their Eyes*; *this* was the one he wanted to scream out on national television, but he was told by the producers it was *too heavy*. The music stopped Rob in his Chucks and he stared, his eyes wide and bright. It was indeed a different world—*his* world, one he always hoped existed somewhere. Dark, smoky, loud, and thanks to the bouncers blocking the stairs, relatively zombie-free. Somehow, it seemed less dangerous with the lights out. Maybe Kurt had a point? Rob soaked it all in. This was what he wanted, and it was right here in his home town! The events of the night whirled through his mind: the despair, the peculiar moments of happiness, the temptation, hope, and moral dilemma. Perhaps this was purgatory—being shown the bad and the good, the what-could-be and what-might-have-been? Somehow, though, he always expected the good to be up and the bad to be down, but he guessed that depended on your point of view... or your understanding of the theological implications in *Bill and Ted's Bogus Journey*. But these were all thoughts for later, when Rob had time to process. Right now, in this moment, he was thinking one thing and one thing only: *here I am now, entertain me!*

Damn right!

The dance floor was right at the back of the main room, rammed with black and green-clad dancers who had no clue anything was wrong. They were all in for Krist Novoselic's epic bass line, Dave Grohl's pounding drums, and Kurt Cobain's screaming vocals. The song lifted people, drove them to the dance floor in a frenzy, while upstairs, people died. There was chaos and there was dancing. There was death and there was disco. It was contagious, and Rob wanted in. There was nothing he could do about the zombies, not here. Not now. There had been at least three people upstairs taking the drugs, and God knows how many more in town. It was futile. They were all fucked. If this was the end of the world, he might never get an opportunity like this again.

Oh well, never mind.

Rob raced onto the dance floor and danced to the music he loved in a club he wished he knew about before shuffling off the mortal coil. He jumped and bounced around, singing at the top of his voice with complete abandon. There was no childish fear of making a nob of himself, none of that boys-on-one-side-of-the-hall, girls-on-the-other, school-disco shit. Rob was dead. He couldn't change that, but there was music in his afterlife, and it was excellent! Music that made him, even just for a short time, *feel* something else.

It was a *very* short time.

Kurt Cobain saw to that.

As the gentle twang of the second verse kicked in, the lyrics and their meaning filtered through the fog of what might once have been adrenaline, and Rob opened his eyes while the people around him danced and sang as if in slow motion. He looked at them. Really looked at them. The innocent. The friends. Those smiling with their eyes closed, completely lost in the music, reveling in it as the bass thundered through their bodies. Those who had found their place and their people, and had no idea that the club they hated so much upstairs was about to rain Burberry-clad zombies on them and fuck everything up. Rob saw a girl fall, exhausted, into her boyfriend's arms, her hair wet and her face glowing as he laughed and held her tight. He noticed the Japanese tattoo on her breast and wondered how much it hurt. In a dark corner, he saw two guys with black hair, black nails, and black eyeliner share a quick, passionate kiss and hold each other's hands, laughing and looking thrilled and embarrassed at the same time. He saw people he recognised from school and people he didn't. All of them loving life. All of them dancing so close to the end of it. Oblivious.

He couldn't just sit back and do nothing.

Rob peered through the crowd and saw a bouncer desperately holding the door against a struggling horde from upstairs. He didn't know if the people pushing on the other side were alive or dead, but as Kurt screamed "a denial" over and over, Rob made up his mind. He was dead, but his conscience, it seemed, was very much alive.

He had to stop the music. He had to give them a chance.

Rob moved over to the DJ booth, concentrated hard, and like Jesus in a temple, flipped the fuck out of the tables.

Song 2

Some songs are made for running, and Rob couldn't shake the screaming, fuzzy bass of Blur's 'Song 2' as he raced along the Stray. The familiar chords had burst in to rapturous screams just before he summoned everything he had to destroy the DJ booth and ultimately wind up back at the car park.

The run through the town was different this time. For one thing, it was shorter; the club being much closer than the police station. But the main difference was the empty streets and the orange glow of the flaring stack. It lit the sky again in a hellscape of bright orange, smothering the ineffectual lights of the various emergency vehicles that remained where they had been abandoned, many now on fire. There were no people—no living people anyway. The beach park was deserted. The Coast Road was deserted. Lord Street was deserted. There were bodies littered here and there—those who had been fed upon by so many that the word "body" was more habit than accurate description. As he ran, Rob became aware of a noise, not unlike the ocean itself: a shifting, undulating hiss that grew louder the closer he got to the club.

He turned the corner near St Peter's Church and stopped in his tracks, coincidentally right outside the God shop. He glanced in the window for a moment and saw sun-bleached covers of Christian magazines and books sporting titles like *Saved* and *He is Risen,* but it wasn't religion that stopped him—it was the lack of it.

At the top of the road, moving along the high street, were the undead.

Finally, unmistakably, a horde. There were hundreds, all heading in the same direction, their faces turned towards the blazing inferno on the horizon. Rob glanced at the shop once more, and a smiling Jesus stared back from a book called *He has a Plan for You*.

"Care to share?" Rob asked. Jesus said nothing, just smiled knowingly.

The horde shuffled together like rats after the Pied Piper, washing around a food van which, bizarrely, had customers. Two long-haired stoners leaned against the open hatch, waiting patiently for pie and peas that was never going to come. Rob pushed on, darting in and out of the walking dead, searching for his body, and desperately trying to think of something he could do that might make a difference. Sure, he had the plan. Pauline's plan. Push the bugger into the ocean, but neither of them had realised just how many zombies there were.[15]

Even if Rob could find himself and managed to steer him to a watery grave, what difference would it make? There were too many. Never mind a drop in the ocean; this was a fart in a jacuzzi.

Rob stopped and the tide flowed through him.

"I should've kept dancing."

In a strange moment of serendipity, Rob sighed and looked up… at the only window with a light still on. Behind the net curtain, a familiar face peered out. It was Pauline. Her eyes were wide, her face framed by the long blonde hair that shone golden in the light from her room. Rob waved but immediately snatched his hand away, hoping Pauline didn't see and wave back, the last thing he wanted was to draw attention to her. One mistake and the whole lot would be beating down her door. Pauline's light went out and the window turned into a black hole. The horde moved on.

As they passed Marks & Spencer, Rob began to pay attention to the way the crowd moved. They were like Boro supporters heading to the Riverside for their weekly disappointment. The horde pulsed and stretched, contracted

---

[15] It perhaps should have occurred to Rob that any old body would do, that it didn't necessarily have to be his, but the human attachment to flesh is powerful, and it never even crossed his mind to give old Mr Aldershot from the Post Office a shove towards the sea.

and expanded, but ultimately stayed together as they made a slow parade, bearing down inexorably on the town clock. They broke around the red-brick tower like water around a lighthouse. The streets were deserted, and the zombies had no stimulus—nothing to follow, no one to lead them on, other than those who were already at the front. As they circled the clock, the leaders bumped into each other, and Rob realised that if they stopped, the mass would simply remain in place, not moving until something drew their attention.

And there it was.

Right at the very front, right in the thick of it.

His body.

"Of course," Rob said with an accepting nod. It seemed like fate on a fateless night, so why fight it? Pauline's plan was a decent one, and at the very least, he should try. No more distractions. It was too dangerous. The zombies were mindless sheep looking for a leader. He would use the shell of who he had once been to lead them all to their deaths. Well, their sort of deaths. Again. Maybe. He would *make* his zombie the Alpha.

Rob knew he would have to be careful. Too much, and he'd end up back on the Stray, but if he gave it a little poke here and a little prod there—just enough of a shove to gather momentum—he reckoned the others would follow. *Pokémon time. Gotta catch them all.* A thrill of excitement rippled through him.

Robbie Neville. King of the Dead. The Saviour of Redcar.

As far as ideas went, it was pretty fucking rock and roll.

Love is the Law

As it turned out, saving the world was pretty bloody boring. It ultimately boiled down to the occasional light prod of an idiot who tried to wander away from hundreds of other idiots. It took twenty minutes just to get them into Queen Street, heading slowly towards the outskirts of town. Rob spent a good five of those minutes scooping the stragglers away from the brightly lit window of Blockbuster videos.

The Sixth Sense. Out now.

Sod off.

He stared at Bruce Willis for a moment before running to catch up with the front. At least Rob knew he was dead. And at least now he knew where he was going. He could almost lay back and enjoy the ride.

Rob whistled The Seahorses' 'Love is the Law' to pass the time, mentally ripping the insanely long guitar solo, closing his eyes and running his fingers over an imaginary fretboard. Around him, the zombies provided constant backing vocals to his air guitar.

They were so damn slow.

Not even John Squire's epic solo was long enough to get him to the other end of Queen Street. The only moment of excitement came when a door opened among the terraced houses and a young man stepped outside to light a suspicious-looking cigarette. He had what Rob's mum would politely call *eyes like piss-holes in the snow,* and the way he slowly blinked at the moaning mob was indication enough to Rob that the man was so stoned he probably wouldn't remember much of this in the morning anyway... if he lived. Three of the shuffling mortally challenged noticed the young man and headed towards him, shifting the trajectory of the whole mob behind them. And here, amidst his boredom, Rob suddenly had a moral dilemma on his hands. Did he run back and shove the zombies away, hoping to spare this one man's life, or did he just keep going and chalk it up to one more sad loss in a night of sad losses? What if, by leaving the head of the horde to save the silly little stoner, he let, say, five innocent children die?[16] The greatest good for the greatest number of people. Was that really what it boiled down to?

No. sod that.

Rob ran back and stepped in front of the man just as the first zombie lifted its arms towards him. He concentrated, lifted his own arms, and shoved. There was enough contact to spin the shuffling body away, and it fell back into the horde, carrying the other two with it.

"Blimey," said the stoner, in an accent that did not belong in this small northern town. "Cheers, old bean."

"Don't mention it," Rob said, and re-joined the front of the horde.

He was nearing the end of Queen Street before he realised the man had spoken to him, but by then it was too late to go back. He was stuck in the monotony of shove, pause, follow, shove, pause, follow. They were heading towards the golf course, crossing the road near his mam's favourite fish and chip shop, almost at the abandoned site of the old leisure centre.

It was then that Rob finally stopped, right in the middle of the road, and it had nothing to do with the stoner.

His mam.

When Rob was younger, his mam and nanna used to walk to 'Keep Fit' every Thursday at the Leisure Centre, only to undo all their good work on the way home by ducking into the chippy and ordering large bags of chips, scraps and two tubs of curry sauce. To Rob, it looked like cat sick, but right

---

[16] There were no children at the other end of the moon-lit Queen Street, but as Rob was having a night of it—the whole *'life flashing before the eyes'* thing—he couldn't help but think back to school. He even remembered what utilitarianism meant. Not that he thought it would come in handy in the afterlife, but for that matter, neither would Ox-bow lakes, and they are undeniably excellent.

now it was all he could think of. His mam and curry sauce. His mam and nanna. His mam. His mam and dad.

An idea struck him like a slap on a cold day. Suddenly, he was full of them—Mr Motivator. This one came to him as an ambulance raced through the horde, lights flashing and siren blasting through the night. It took him a good ten minutes to get all the zombies back on track and heading in the right direction after it had gone, but the fact there were still living, breathing people out there, doing their best to help others, shone in his mind like a bright star. He had seen the determination on the face of the driver as she barrelled the van through the crowd. That woman knew what was going on. She was a paramedic, and yet she hadn't stopped or even slowed down for the mass of the undead. The red and black smears across the road were testament to that. She knew they were beyond help; she knew this was a fight, and she acted. The world had not stopped spinning.

It had *not* stopped spinning!

Rob was tired. He was wearing thin, but the zombies had the open ground of the golf course ahead of them, and beyond that, the long stretch of wilderness that ran parallel to the steelworks. It would take them ages to get across there. If he ran, and if he timed it right, he would have this one chance.

One chance to say goodbye to his parents.

It's The End Of The World As We Know It (And I Feel Fine)

The Stead Hospital was close—just on the other side of the cricket ground, past the Lobster pub and a long line of houses that looked like they should be in Bath or London, not Redcar. Tall, white, posh. Rob figured he'd run through the cricket ground, check the hospital, and race back through Coatham, rejoining the horde on the other side. It wasn't much of a detour, and with the fact he could run through buildings, he figured everything would be *kushti*.

What he didn't factor in was the delay caused by a group of men playing cricket in the nude.

Life, indeed, goes on.

Rob stumbled to a halt at mid-wicket and stared in wonder. There were at least thirty men, completely oblivious to the carnage, clearly hammered, and enjoying a game of cricket in the nuddy. Oh sure, the pace was slightly off, but that's to be expected when you're swinging low in the crease. A man ran in and bowled a dodgy spin, the familiar thunk of ball on wood echoing in the night as the batsman connected. A fielder snatched the ball off the bounce, fell, rolled, and returned it to the wicketkeeper, all while holding his beer high—safely un-spilt. The men burst into spontaneous applause, and the fielder celebrated by draining the rest of the can. The whole scene was an utterly surreal break in a night of horrors. With any luck, Rob thought, these men would go home completely unaware of the tragedy that had befallen the town. The night would not be remembered for death and unspeakable violence, but for the enjoyment of playing cricket in the buff and laughing at your mate's willy as he floundered for a catch.

Rob darted through the fence near the clubhouse and onto the road beyond. The Stead hospital lay ahead, down the street near the train tracks. He had no idea if his parents would even be there, but he had to check. At the very least, it should only take a few minutes to run through the emergency rooms before racing back to the horde.

As it turned out, it didn't even take that long.

They were both there, tears pouring from his mam's eyes as she held grimly onto her husband's remaining hand. Rob found them mid-conversation in the first room he checked.

"No, love," his dad tried to explain. "I don't know how, but it was our Rob who saved me. He was there, but—"

"But you think he's dead?"

There was a long pause while they both cried. The juxtaposition from naked cricket to life-altering sorrow was not lost on Rob. If he had a heart, it would have broken for his parents' pain.

"I'm sorry. I don't know… I don't know what else to say."

"You've never lied to me, love. Never. Not once. But please, *please* tell me you're lying now!" The pain in his mam's voice was more than Rob could bear. He reached out and she shivered as his hand passed through her shoulder. He cried then. What else could he do? Some emotions are more powerful than biology. Tears fell from his eyes and landed on the floor.

His mam noticed.

She saw the plink of moisture hit the bleached surface, shining in the reflection of the dim lights before vanishing. She shivered again, turning from her husband.

"Rob?" she asked. Because a mother always knows.

"I'm here, Mam." Rob cried and tried to hug her. As he did, her shiver became something else. Rob's mam knew her boy was there. She also knew—the two thoughts piling one on top of the other leaving no room to breathe—that he was truly dead. The knowledge crushed her, and her legs buckled beneath the weight of a reality she couldn't bear. Rob's mam fell to the floor and cried in despair. The ghost of her dead son tried to hold her and comfort her but all he felt was her pain.

"I'm here, Mam," he cried. "I'm so sorry."

"Don't," she replied. "Don't say sorry, darling. I'm sorry. I wasn't there. I didn't protect you."

Rob's dad fell from the gurney and crashed to the floor beside his wife, throwing his arms around her, unknowingly gathering his son in his embrace. The three of them sat on the floor and sobbed.

"He's here isn't he," his father said. It wasn't a question.

Rob's mam sobbed her heart out as it ripped in two, but she knew somehow, in some way that only a mother can, that her boy still needed her.

"Whatever it is you have to do, son," she said. "You do it. My baby boy. I love you. We both love you. You do what you need to do. We'll never stop loving you. We'll meet you on the other side. We'll never let you go."

That was too much for Rob. His parents clung to each other in desperation and sorrow, and he fled, racing into the night with the words of his mother echoing in his mind.

It was time to bring an end to this ridiculous night.

It was time to find his way to the other side.

If You Tolerate This Your Children Will Be Next

Rob raced through the streets with a pain in his chest that did not belong. Only true sorrow can cut through mind, body, and soul. He ran as if he was trying to outrun himself and barely noticed all the houses he careened through. There were no people. It was late and they were asleep, but there was an old man in the church at Coatham, another of those Anglican relics littering the country with their beautiful gothic architecture. Rob wondered how long they would remain. How long before people realised the truth that the promised salvation of the afterlife was complete bollocks? How long could religion maintain dominance when there were only a handful of people in the pews but countless masses in the bars? His mind threw images at him from his youth as a boy scout, marching up the aisle with the troop flag wedged into a leather holder on his waist, his sleeve of badges on proud display. Twenty-seven in total. Robert Neville. Ninth Redcar Scout troop. He remembered it well. He ran on. Through the church and across the scout hall. It felt like he was retracing his own life on the map of the town he grew up in. His uncle had lived on the corner just near the roundabout. He had his first driving lesson just over the bridge. He caught the train to Middlesbrough with his mam on those tracks. Locke Park was just over there. He played there as a kid and experimented there as a teen. It was all too hard to bear, and so Rob ignored it, choosing instead to run through the tall houses on Coatham Road and out through the sheds and garages in the back lanes.

As soon as Rob crossed the last wall, he heard it, the hiss and hum of the horde. They were right there, on the golf course, some struggling in the rough, but the whole lot moving inexorably towards the flaring stacks to the north. Rob stopped. There was no need to catch his breath, he had none, but he did smile. His mam was right, he had something to do. He saw his own body leading the herd and realised that this was probably it, this was his big moment, his purpose. Sod *Stars in Their Eyes*. Sod five minutes of fame. Sod getting off with Vikki Abraham in the back of a car. He might be dead, but he could still make a difference. He was going to save the town. Perhaps then he would be set free? Perhaps he was wrong about religion after all?

With the town at his back, Rob walked towards the dead.

There were people he loved here. *He* loved it here. It didn't matter that he was dead, there were many who weren't.

We are judged by what we walk past.

Rob didn't get it before—about the town. He thought it was a shithole. He just wanted to escape, to get out and live the life of a rock star, but he understood now the way the locals talked about the place, the way his parents did. It was home, and he was going to save it!

And then, just as Rob was feeling suitably righteous, everything slowed, and the horde shuffled to a halt.

Because even the emotional impetus of an epiphanic realisation can be quite easily fucked on by logistics.

Or a fence.

Getting Better

Majuba Road cut the golf course in two, and the only way across was via a small gate in the iron railings. A gate with a simple latch. The zombies hit the barrier and turned, each body mindlessly following those in front without so much as a thought of independence.

But this was it. His moment.

Rob stepped up.

He knew it would take all his concentration, but his new conviction came with a steely determination. He made his way through the horde and reached the gate. He gathered himself, raised his finger to the latch, and pushed.

Nothing happened.

Rob tried again.

Nothing continued to happen.

The gate didn't move. In fact, it didn't budge a smegging inch, but Rob felt the weariness wash over him as though he had been bench-pressing dead guys. The now tell-tale signs that he might soon wink out of existence and reappear a few miles away flickered around the edges like the slow rise of absinthe. Rob pushed again, but it was no use. His hand slipped right through. He yelled out in desperation, trying to grip the handle with both hands but they just wouldn't take. The zombies walked blindly into the fence and followed the others along the perimeter, heading back. Rob swore and had another little tantrum, screaming and shouting into the void.

"It's done," he sobbed. "It's over. The whole town is fucked."

"Not the whole town."

Rob looked up in shock.
A zombie looked back at him.
A zombie in a red dress and a leather jacket.
Pauline was back, and she was dead.

Pretend We're Dead

Pauline stepped closer to Rob and ripped her face off. He would have fainted if he could.

"What the fuck? Is that... did you... what the fuck?"

"Oh, this?" she said, holding up the mask, its slack features hanging low. "Fancy dress, sweetie."

"Thank God! I thought you'd skinned one of them!"

"Christ on a bike, love. That's a bit strong. You have had a night, haven't you? Imagine wearing a dead person's skin! I'm not Buffalo Bill!"

"Sorry. I—"

"The closest I'll get to wearing skin is this fabulous leather jacket," she said with a small twirl. "We're going to have to whisper, though, they're getting a tad suspicious."

Pauline was right. Some of the zombies had stopped and were staring at her, with, let's be honest, hungry eyes. She pulled the mask into place and shifted the set of her body. One shoulder dropped, and she moaned. The zombies lost interest, buffeted by the hundreds still washing up against the fence.

"I'll open these gates," she said in a quiet voice. "You're going to have to go back and steer the stragglers. Can you do that?"

"Yes," Rob said. "I get tired, but I've got it under control. The fence though... the gate... I couldn't..."

"You're probably just tired, sweetie. A little bit of performance anxiety. It happens to the best of us. Come along, get a shufty on. I don't want to be out here all night." Pauline opened the gate and stepped into the quiet road. She moved slowly and deliberately, waiting for enough of the undead to follow her through the gap before moving to the gate on the opposite side of the road.

What a woman, Rob thought. Then he turned his attention to the horde.

Individuals and small groups had broken free and were scattered all over the golf course. It was like *One Man and His Dog,* only Rob didn't have a dog, and his sheep were a bit more bitey. He ran as fast as he could, prodding here and poking there—just enough to turn a shoulder and cause the mindless to move. A little nudge, and they followed the mob happily enough, but there were so many! Just when he thought he had them all, another would break free and go for a wander. He swore as he ran, repeating the process over and over until the crowd eventually began to thin, funneling through the gate until, finally, he ushered the last one through just as the first hint of grey teased the horizon.

"That'll do, pig," Rob said. "That'll do."

It was only when he finished and followed the last zombie that he realised the error—they were going the wrong way.

Change

"You're going the wrong way!" Rob shouted, racing through the horde. The exertion had given him a headache. That wasn't fair—he was pretty sure they didn't have paracetamol in the afterlife. He was angry by the time he got to Pauline, but when he saw the look on her face, he felt instantly guilty.

Headaches and guilt—a winning combination.

Pauline was terrified. Rob could see the fear and strain in her eyes through the rubber mask. The perfect make-up smudged all to hell. It was different for her. Any one of the hundreds of snarling creatures would happily rip her apart if she so much as faltered.

"I'm sorry," he said, "but… the sea. Why aren't we moving towards the sea?"

"Caravans," she whispered, not daring to take her eyes off the dark dunes as she moved, step by careful step. One slip, one stocking caught in a patch of grass, one twisted ankle, and it was all over. Thankfully, Pauline had ditched the high heels for a sturdy pair of Doc Martens.[17]

"What do you mean?" he asked.

"The caravan park is over there," she hissed. "Right along the edge of the golf course. Can't risk it." The nearest zombie groaned, and they heard the snap of teeth. It was horrible. Rob saw Pauline wince. She'd put up with that since she left her flat.

---

[17] With bright red laces to match the dress, of course. She might be practical, but she was also fucking fabulous.

"What do we do?"

The steelworks loomed ahead, huge and dominating the landscape as it always had, the silhouette large and black against the flaring stacks.

"Keep going to the river," she said. "It's a bloody long way, though." Another zombie snapped, and Pauline choked back a gasp. "Your friend is over there," she added, composing herself with an effort and pointing. Rob turned. It was hard to pick individuals in the shifting sea of dark heads, but a familiar haircut caught his eye.

"Hey bud," he waved at himself and felt like a nobhead, but then the burning stack flared violently again, painting the world orange.

Ahead, the blast furnace stood out like a giant beast against the glow. It was huge—an iconic part of the local landscape that always put Rob in mind of Ted Hugh's *Iron Giant*, kind of friendly in a way. But right now, it towered over them like a skeleton, a devil of steel and iron.

The zombies stared at the looming behemoth like a crowd on bonfire night. The only thing missing was the obligatory oohs and aahs beneath exploding fireworks. Instead, there were groans and growls, and the occasional fart. In the bright light, individual faces stood out to Rob. He recognised people—locals who had patterned his life in some way or another. They all played their parts. There was the man from the Wine Lodge. And the disco man! His mam's favourite Avon Lady was in there as well; she'd be appalled at the state of her face. There were others—teachers, classmates, nightclubbers, bus drivers, police officers and that wanker who pushed the trolleys at the supermarket who always shouted at the kids for cycling through the car park. None of them deserved this. Not even trolley wanker.

The flaring stack grew brighter, casting dancing shadows over the horde and reaching out across the golf course. Rob looked at the town: the boating lake, the Mungle Jungle, the long row of houses leading to the beach. This was home... this was...

The flare flickered and died. The zombies vanished as the world descended into darkness.

Black Hole Sun

Pauline let out a small noise as the light was sucked from the world. The dunes and golf course vanished instantly, and it was suddenly impossible to make out anything as shapes danced in front of her eyes. She stumbled once, then twice. Rob caught her arm and pushed her back to her feet, gasping from the effort.

"Thank you," she said in the dark. "Are you okay?"

"I'm alright," he nodded, "keep moving."

He wasn't alright. That had cost him. He felt weak, faint, spread too thin. He concentrated on his breathing and tried to stay in control, stumbling through a sandpit. He blinked and blinked. How could he have dancing lights in front of his eyes when he didn't have eyes? It wasn't fair, but it wasn't the worst thing. In the absence of light, the noise of the horde magnified, each slather and snap from an invisible mouth a punctuation mark in a sentence of dread.

Rob looked to his right. There was definitely a smudge of grey on the horizon, but it was about as effective as trying to play a Gameboy at night. There were shapes, sure, but he was buggered if he could make them out.

Then he tripped, and the fear overwhelmed him. Rob felt the mass of bodies behind him—leaning, reaching, inexorable and relentless. It didn't matter if you were dead; being on the ground in front of a crowd was terrifying. It was a fear he'd had since he was a kid, a fear of being crushed. Rob choked down a cry and scrambled after Pauline. At least the dead were even worse on their feet than him; the susurrus of the shuffling and groaning bodies was punctuated by the frequent thud, thud, thud of faces hitting the ground. *Thank God they can't run,* Rob thought. But there was something about the relentlessness, the never-ending march of the horde, that was scary enough. Rob wasn't even sure driving them into the water would do the trick; they'd probably just get all bloated and fuck up the fish.

The music of the world filtered through slowly, weaving into the hiss and sough of the horde. The roll of the distant tide, the strangled call of birds who woke up, saw the dead, and thought better of it, the wail of emergency vehicles, and the general clamour of a world stretching its legs. But always, always, was the noise of the horde itself. The slip, the shift, the slow murmur of bodies defying logic and biology. The farts and the burps as gasses built and escaped via unprecedented movement, and the occasional thump as they tripped in the rough and fell flat on their face. The darkness magnified it all, amplified it.

A danger you can't see can be far worse than one you can. Rob was overwhelmed.

Then Pauline took control.

"This way, sweeties! This way!" she called, her voice carrying that musical feminine lilt but punctuated by a deeper growl as she struggled through the thick grass. "Follow your Aunty Pauline—*you undead wankers! Ruined my dress!*—Come along, my darlings!"

The growl of the horde rose as they heard Pauline and tried to reach her. They were far beyond the lights of the caravan park now and a sliver of hope rose in Rob. It was working, they were moving, filtering onto the fairway in an orderly line. He'd seen queues at the Post Office on pension day less organised than this.

British zombies. The best in the business.

"You're doing it!" he called out. "Keep going!"

Pauline began to sing, her voice strong and powerful in the predawn light. Dolly Parton. '9 to 5.'

"Jesus Christ!" Rob laughed.

"Nope. Just Pauline," she shouted back. "Though I'd kill for his abs."

It almost worked.

Almost.

But the world apparently did not want to give them a break. The stack flared once again, and the zombies turned towards the light.

The great fear of firefighters is that the wind will change direction. A fire is manageable while it blows one way; they can meet it head-on, direct it, steer it, end it, but if the wind changes and hits a fire from the side, it's shit creek time. Instantly, the single-file line of patient pensioners turned into a ragged mob, crossing the golf course like Blackadder crossing No Man's Land. Ahead lay the houses and buildings of Warrenby and the blast furnace itself. Rob and Pauline stood on a dune and watched, utterly helpless. The beach was behind them. The water was in sight. They had been so close!

Pauline pulled the rubber mask off, wiped her face with her hands, and ran her fingers through her hair.

"Well... bum," she said.

Her eyes were hard and set. There was fear there, but something else as well—something Rob didn't like. She gathered her hair, pulling it up behind her head. She looked at Rob, locking eyes with him. She saw the translucency from the effort it took to steady her and steer the dead, the fear and concern, and the underlying care and affection. Pauline lifted a hand to Rob's face and smiled. She saw right through him.

"Get the stragglers if you can, sweetie."

"What? I don't—"

"What a way to make a living," she said, and ran.

Bronzed legs glistened in the flare as Pauline hitched up her dress and legged it over the dunes and bunkers. She hit the first zombie in the back, sending it tumbling away, and roared a battle cry more Broadway than *Braveheart*, but she kept going, shouldering another, then another. Just when Rob thought she'd break through the line she turned back and kept going, always moving, always shoving. Pauline danced on the highest dune and kicked her legs out in a dazzling can-can, then turned away, the horde following, funnelling after her. Rob watched in stunned silence; then, finally, he got to work.[18]

---

[18] To be fair, Pauline was distractingly fabulous!

As Pauline led the horde like the leader of the most bizarre Notting Hill Carnival, Rob ran around the edges, doing his best *Babe* impression: nudging, suggesting, shoving where he could, finding the stragglers and getting them back into line. The running itself didn't bother him. It hadn't bothered him all night. But every time he touched a zombie, every time he concentrated enough to give someone a shove, it hurt. He could feel the desire to let go, the pull that would make him vanish and wake up on the other side of town. Twice now it had happened, and he had no idea how much time passed between the moment the lights went out and when he returned. There was no time for that, though. No time at all. There were too many zombies heading in the wrong direction, too many threats.

He kept going. Faster and faster. Pushing himself as hard as he could—shoving, nudging, and, in some places, kicking. It seemed to take an eternity, and by the time it ended, Rob's whole being pulsed with pain. He stopped and screamed, feeling the blackness closing in but forcing it away. There was one more.

Of course, there was one more.

"It had to be you," he gasped.

Rob struggled after himself, slowly closing the gap as his body moved towards a wire-mesh fence. His legs were heavy, his chest tight. Whatever the spiritual equivalent of lactic acid was, he was drowning in it, but he couldn't stop. To his horror, he saw an open gate and, inside, the thing that had drawn his body's attention; a barking dog straining at the end of a long chain. He heard the commotion, though in some odd magic of distance and time, he saw the dog's jaw open before he heard the noise. Rob put his head down and ran but staggered as the grass gave way to a bunker. He was exhausted, nearly done. The darkness closed in, but Rob railed against it. "Ghosts shouldn't get knackered!" he gasped and dragged himself on. He had to. He couldn't let his zombie eat a dog! What kind of fucking hell on earth exists where a zombie eats a dog?

But his body was at the fence, moving and groaning as the barks grew frantic, and no matter how fast Rob ran, it just wasn't fast enough. He was trapped in a dream, and there was nothing he could do to stop it.

The zombie found the open gate while Rob was still thirty feet away.

The dog strained and howled, lifting itself on the lead as it pulled.

Twenty feet.

It was a German Shepherd, a big, beautiful Alsatian.

Ten feet.

As the zombie moved closer, Rob saw the moment the dog's instincts flicked a switch. It snapped off a bark mid-sentence and turned, racing to the other end of the chain, tail tucked, desperate to get away, but there was nowhere to go.

Rob fell through the fence as the zombie reached out. A man appeared in a doorway. There was a scream, and Rob rugby tackled himself into a bin.

Choose Life

Car Park. Bus. High Street. Golf club. Vikki. Wayne. Dad. Choose disco. Choose Pauline. Choose life. If Rob could have chosen anything, it would have been the ability to teleport. Though, right now, he'd settle for faster bloody legs! The flare had stopped when he was somewhere near the Regent Cinema, racing past the strange building jutting into the sea. He was beyond tired. There was no time to rest. It was like trying to complete *Ghosts N Goblins* on the NES with one life left. The slightest knock, the slightest mistake and he'd be back at the start.

As he climbed the first dune of the golf course, he knew before he got to the top that he was already too late. Rob looked down. The snaking mass of zombies was there, much further away, still moving in line. Only now, instead of heading out to the sea, they made a straight run towards the blast furnace.

"No!" Rob gasped. They'd failed. It was all over. Pauline would never have led them there. Even this early in the morning, there would be hundreds of people on-site.

He struggled on; he had to know. But first, the dog.

Rob slowed as he approached the open fence. His body was there, on its knees, feeding. He felt a rage build within him that ripped through his ethereal body like electricity. It was lightning—hot, fierce, angry. He screamed at himself and didn't even register when the head of the zombie snapped up and turned those cold, dead eyes on him. He didn't look so cool anymore. The veneer of the rock star was gone. Someone had put up a hell of a fight. Rob's eye was a bloody mess, and his nose was broken. The face had been ripped at the cheek, and the left ear hung loose, but he was still moving, the virus still in him, still giving him… life. Rob stalked across the yard, taking it all in—the body, the broken chain, the blood—and suddenly he didn't care. He felt nothing but hate and contempt for himself. Even if there was a way to climb back inside, to come back, he wouldn't take it. Not now. Not after everything it had done.

Rob screamed and punched himself in the face.

It was a good punch. It had none of the restrictions of dreams or muscle memory. The head snapped back, and the body crashed into the iron shed, but it wasn't enough. Rob grabbed his body by the throat and dragged it violently away from the half-eaten corpse. He pulled it through the yard and flung it at the feet of the walking dead. His body shuffled and twitched, but the others stepped on it, trampled it. The hands reached out, and the creature growled and moaned, but Rob stalked away. He didn't care anymore, not about himself, not about the horde, but he had to know what happened to Pauline, to his friend. The anger sustained him, kept him going, made him strong. The dark shadows were pushed to the edges, and he didn't question it. He let the anger build.

The zombies moved through a broken fence, crossing the threshold from green grass to dirt and iron. Rob followed, simmering, searching. Through the sheds, through the pipes and shafts, through the muddy waters that reminded him of *Robocop*. And then he saw her—a flash of red, a flash of blonde. Pauline. At the front of the line. Shuffling. Head bent.

Rob fell to his knees and wept for a woman he barely knew, as around him the zombies shuffled ever onwards. He felt the tears again. Like the anger that washed through him, the sadness did too—the sorrow of all the loss. He blinked away moisture that made no sense and saw a flash of red, but it was higher now, rising above the heads of the dead and still climbing. He blinked again and wiped his eyes, standing among the shuffling masses. Pauline was halfway up a set of stairs, twisting and turning in rising levels, the zombies following after. She was Donkey Kong; they were Mario. Rob traced the stairs to the top and felt a wave of nausea as the huge structure loomed above. It was massive—a great conveyor rising in a long slope from the ground to the blast furnace. That was still a long way off, far to the right, but impossibly huge, like a monster in the night. The stairs though—those huge, MC Escher, industrial steps—they ran a hundred feet into the sky to the conveyor. Rob had spent many a blissful hour in Lakes Primary School colouring cross-sections of the furnace and he knew the ramp fed fuel from the ground to the top, running it up to the blast furnace, and dropping it into the fire far below. Those little drawings gave no idea of scale. It was massive. Monstrous. A playground slide for giants. Rob watched in stunned silence as one by one the horde followed Pauline's lead and took faltering steps onto the black iron staircase, snaking their way up, back and forth, trailing the woman in the red dress as though she was David Bowie in *Labyrinth*. He couldn't believe what he was seeing, but finally, as the anger and shock subsided, the pieces of the puzzle fell into place.

Rob burst out laughing, and Pauline heard. Even from this distance, their eyes locked, and Rob could see the sparkle behind the rubber mask.

"Cooee!" she called out, and a zombie grabbed her by the ankle.

Killing In The Name

Rob raced up the steps, two, three at a time, shoving bodies out the way. Each hit was like an electric shock, but it was different from before; he didn't feel weak. If anything, he felt stronger.

"Fuck you!" he cried as he swung himself up the steps and shouldered a dead bin-man in the chest. The man went spinning over the railing to the ground far below, where he got up and calmly rejoined the queue. Those Rob didn't hit, he ran right through, each one washing over him like cold rain. He was exhilarated; he felt great. But above him, Pauline was in a desperate scrap. She cried, kicked, and punched, but the zombie's grip was like iron, and it was all she could do to keep the snapping teeth away while the others piled up behind. The mask tore from her face and fell through the railings, tumbling to the earth like an autumn fall in hell. There were two on her now, three, and a fourth clambering over their backs to reach out for fresh meat. Pauline fought desperately, and then her eyes widened as Rob's face appeared. She could see right through him, the last remaining stars glimmering through his face.

Rob grabbed the first zombie in a headlock and forced it back, roaring his own battle cry. Somewhere in the deep recesses of his mind, in those memories of reading fantasy novels by torchlight underneath his *A-Team* bed sheets, he thrilled at the fact he finally got to have a war cry. Rage Against the Machine's 'Killing in the Name' probably wasn't what his younger self had in mind, but it worked for him.[19]

"Fluff you! I won't do what you ask me!" he cried as he flung the dead bus driver down the stairs, skittling three others on the way.

"Fluff you! I won't do what you ask me!"

Another followed. A woman in a small skirt this time with a giant bite mark on her thigh. He punched an old lady in the back of the head, and it didn't even register.

"Fluff you! I won't do what you ask me!"

Finally, Rob could see the zombie whose hand still gripped Pauline's Doc Martens, and he raised his foot.

"Mother fluffer!"

Rob screamed the end of the song and brought his Converse-clad spiritual foot down in a phantom kerb stomp as savage as *American History X*. The wrist snapped against the iron step and tore away as easily as a brittle branch leaning against a tree. Every kid has broken a thousand sticks this way, channeling their inner Daniel LaRusso or Jackie Chan, though sticks don't often spill thick black gunk from both ends. And neither do they have fingers still grasping at bright red laces. Pauline grabbed the hand and yanked it free, throwing it over the edge of the stairs.

"Thank you, sweetie," she said.

"Don't mention it," Rob breathed. His eyes were on fire.

Pauline looked at him. There was concern in that look but also a decent portion of fear. Though, to be fair, anyone who had just witnessed a dead man karate-chop the shit out of other dead people while screaming a Rage Against the Machine song with mam-friendly lyrics could probably be forgiven for being a little nervous.

"You're..." she reached out to pat his cheek and her hand passed right through. Rob didn't even flinch. "You've got a good voice," she said, and moved around the stairs as the unrelenting horde continued their march to the heavens, spurred on by the commotion.

---

[19] The lyrics here will be edited accordingly as someone's mam says he swears too much. Honestly, that's the reason. It has nothing to do with copyright laws.

"Thank you," Rob said.

"I watched you on *Stars in Their Eyes*, you know, after you left. I'd taped it." Pauline breathed heavily as she climbed, her magnificent legs straining, her hands shaking as she shifted her grip with each step. Below them, the zombies followed, all back on their feet now, all focused on the woman in the red dress. "You were great."

"Oh," Rob said. He couldn't think of anything else, his mind was in tatters, not helped by the ridiculous height. *Of all the things to be scared of when you're dead, vertigo shouldn't be one,* he thought. He walked on, keeping his gaze focused on Pauline.

"You look a lot like him, you know. Kurt Cobain."

"The make-up helped."

"Make-up isn't all it's cracked up to be," she said. "It often hides who we really are. Not for me of course, but then, I'm special." She laughed then, but it was a desperate noise punctuated by tears. Rob got a good look at Pauline as they climbed. She was covered in scratches, bruises, and blood. *They never get that right in the movies,* he thought. *Everyone just seems to plough on without a hair out of place.* Pauline had been fighting for her life. It showed.

"Pauline, I—"

"I mean you look like him now," she said. "When he was young. Before the drugs. Such a handsome boy."

She was just talking for the sake of talking, to have some company in what she no doubt expected to be the last moments of her life. Rob knew it and couldn't for the life of him fathom where the courage came from.

"Pauline, what are you doing?"

The magnificent woman laughed again, then straightened her back and wiped her eyes. They were at the end. A door sat in the side of the conveyor housing. Pauline turned to Rob and pulled a set of keys from her leather jacket.

"Sweetie, I'm going to kill the dead and save the world. And no one is ever going to know." Pauline opened the door, and the noise of the moving conveyor filled the world with thunder. It was huge and monstrous, a great machine feeding a beast.

"How?" Rob shouted over the din.

"That furnace is over a thousand degrees," Pauline said, pointing into the dark. "We just need to get them through the door. The conveyor will take care of the rest."

She gasped suddenly, painfully, and a great sob wracked her body. She fought hard to control it, sucking in air and hissing it out between clenched teeth. She turned to Rob and smiled as the nearest zombie reached the top of the stairs. "You just make sure of something, sweetie."

"What? What is it?"

Pauline looked at him, and her eyes grew soft. She ran her fingers through her long blonde hair and tucked a loose strand behind her ear. Then she scratched the stubble on her chin and smiled.

"Keep them coming," she said. Then, turning like a dancer, she grabbed the nearest zombie by the throat and lifted him from the ground with enormous strength. Aunty Pauline—in her boots and bright red dress, with terror in her eyes—dragged the dead man through the door into the dark thunder on the other side.

My Hero

Pauline went to work. She flung the dead man onto the roaring conveyor and watched as he was dragged up the ramp on a pile of coke. She laughed—not because she found it funny, and not because it reminded her of the travelator on *Gladiators*,[20] but because she was bloody terrified and there were hundreds of others to take care of. She turned and planted her feet, grabbing the next zombie by the back of the neck as it poked its head through the opening. He went the way of the first, vanishing into the dark and thunder, dragged away on the churning tide of the River Styx. Pauline risked a glance out of the door and locked eyes with Rob just as the sun rose over the ocean. It was the last she saw of him. In the fresh morning light, Robbie Neville disappeared. Pauline cried out and grabbed the next zombie by the shirt; there was no time to pause, no time to stop and take a breather. It was a never-ending do-si-do, conga-line of the dead. One mistake, one misstep, one slight miscalculation and it would be the end, either through a bite or through falling onto the conveyor herself. There would be no slow road to death like in *Terminator 2.* No cool thumbs up as she sank slowly into the fire. It was over a thousand degrees down there. Pauline would burst into flames before she even got close to the boiling, white-hot mess, which, she hoped, was exactly what was happening to all the undead shits she sent in that direction.

She pulled the next one by the hair, and her heart nearly tore in two as

[20] Jet was her favourite. Not least because she was a local girl.

she recognised the waitress from the strip club, still clad in a leather thong and a black bra, snapping and snarling as she was dragged through the door. "No!" Pauline sobbed, her knees weak, her arms and heart heavy as the body trundled away. Sophie was so lovely. She always treated Pauline just like any other customer, once even fiercely admonishing a group of young men on a stag do, one of whom had dared to call her favourite customer a sissy. "Sissy," Pauline said to herself, as two more snapping dead men followed Sophie up the ramp towards the inevitable drop into hell. "More like Sisyphus."

Pauline knew her Greeks, of course she did—all those gorgeous, bronzed men in short robes. It was the *Jason and the Argonauts* movie she watched as a kid that awakened something deep within her. But Sisyphus, poor Sisyphus, doomed for eternity to push a boulder up a hill. This felt like her fate. She paused for a moment and closed her eyes against the sadness.

It was a moment too long.

Dead fingers caressed her face, and Pauline slapped a clawing hand away in panic, kicking out and losing her balance as the new arrival fell, half on and half off the conveyor, the body rolling and twisting and tumbling as the torso dragged up the pile of coke. Grasping fingers closed around the hem of her dirty red dress and didn't let go.

* * *

Outside, Rob was beginning to panic. The zombies on the stairs were losing interest as the twists and turns of the staircase blocked the sight of the ones below. Without the flash of the bright red dress, and the occasional burst of Dolly, they just didn't have the stimulation to keep going. Rob shouted, but they couldn't hear him. He kicked at the metal railing and stamped his feet, but it was no good, he couldn't produce enough noise. He moved carefully towards the edge and looked down. The zombies who hadn't yet made the steps were slowly branching off, one after the other, the long line becoming ever more ragged. He needed something, anything to draw their attention. The stairs rattled and Rob turned. A zombie appeared and had the answer in his pocket.

It was Wayne.

Wannabe drug lord. Ginger-ninja, a damn sight thinner, and a lot bloodier than before. *Deus Ex Machina* Mark II.

Complete with nunchucks.

Rob gathered himself and concentrated. He'd been here before. Pickpocketing the dead while dead. It wasn't easy, and he knew there would be a price to pay. His anger earlier had done something, changed something, had made him cross a line he might never be able to step back from, but it was worth the risk. Pauline was still in there. Pauline was still fighting. He couldn't let her down.

Rob reached out and took the nunchucks from Wayne's pocket. It was remarkably easy, though part of the lad's hip ripped away and hung like beef jerky. Rob shook them off and the bloody gristle spun away into the dawn.

The zombie watched the floating nunchucks with cold dead eyes, then an almost entirely invisible Rob shoved him through the open door.

Suddenly, Rob was alone as the morning sun rose higher and bathed the steelworks in a golden glow. He looked around. The view was breathtaking, but there were sirens in the distance, and plumes of smoke rising from the town telling their own story. He had to end this. He hefted the nunchucks, one in each hand, and looked at the crowd below.

"Right then, Redcar!" he shouted, smashing the sticks together above his head. "Let's be having you! One, two. One, two, three, four!"

Rob wasn't a particularly great drummer, but what he lacked in technical ability he made up for in enthusiasm.[21] The sticks crashed down on the iron railing with a thunderous beat, leading the guitar riff he heard in his head. He'd never had a lesson to speak of, and he didn't have a drum kit, but a well-organised arrangement of pillows and plastic tubs had allowed him to recreate a set in his bedroom, and he spent many a night pretending to be Dave Grohl, Roger Taylor or, his favourite, Taylor Hawkins. Of course, he was none of those, but every rock star needs to give it a red-hot shot once in a while. He picked a beat he could just about manage, a song he adored, and

[21] Which, for drummers, is nine tenths of the law

like a one-man band, he belted out the lyrics to Foo Fighter's epic 'My Hero' for all he was worth. Zombie heads rose to find the sound of drums, and their feet followed. The staircase wobbled beneath Rob, but he kept going. The wannabe rock star, for one night only, in Redcar with the dead. It was working! Sure, he couldn't see his hands, but it was working. The zombies were coming!

"Pauline!" he shouted. "Hey, Pauline! I'm bringing you some more friends. Get ready!"

The first zombie took a confused swipe at the floating sticks and Rob stepped back, moving towards the door, shifting the drumbeat to the steel walls of the conveyor. He looked into the darkness... into the shadows that moved like thunder.

Pauline was gone.

Rob stepped through, all the while drumming on the door frame, drawing the zombies on, making them follow and stumble over the steps. The first two made it inside, and he moved aside to kick them onto the conveyor, first one, then the other. He blinked. His trusty Chuck Taylor's were almost invisible, but he didn't care about that. Pauline was gone. His hero.

Rob stood alone at the entrance to hell, and the dead came for him.

Alive

Pauline appeared from the darkness like an avenging goddess, because some people are born to make an entrance. She had been dragged halfway to hell and fought tooth and nail to clamber back. A pair of nunchucks floated before her eyes, and she barely blinked, not surprised by anything anymore. They rose triumphantly in the air and counted a beat before smashing a heavy rhythm against the door. Pauline didn't hesitate. She grabbed a zombie and launched it onto the conveyor, working in time to the beat, nodding her head, reaching out, taking a grip, and throwing the dead, while Rob cried in relief that his friend still lived.

Outside, sudden gunfire shattered the dawn.

A black helicopter roared out of the morning sun on thundering rotors, raining bullets up the staircase. Rob stopped his drumming and stepped outside, staring in shock at the line of soldiers making their way across the yard, rifles up, single shots picking off targets. He cheered and pumped his fists in the air as the zombies fell, feeling every inch like Christian Bale in *Empire of the Sun* while the helicopter soared behind the blast furnace. Rob turned to look at Pauline and stared blankly as one more zombie appeared on the last flight of stairs.

He shrugged. Then laughed.

It was him.

Of course it was him.

He had an arm missing where the helicopter's huge bullets had exploded into his shoulder, but he was still moving.

Ever onwards.

They stopped in front of one another. Rob and Rob. The zombie and the ghost. Together again.

"Christ, bud," Rob said. "You've caused some bother tonight."

His body didn't reply. It stared right through him, and Rob suddenly felt exhausted. He just wanted it all to end, and here he was, right on the edge, too tired to be mad, too tired to be sad, too tired to feel. He put his arm around himself and walked through the door to meet Pauline. The zombie snapped at her, but with little enthusiasm. He was just going through the motions. Pauline looked for the real Rob, but she couldn't see him.

"I'm here," he said.

She heard. Her chest heaved as she caught her breath, and tears streaked down her face.

"You're still alive," she said, and Rob couldn't help himself, the lyrics to the famous Pearl Jam song were right there.

"I'm not sure I deserve to be."

"You deserve better than this," she said.

"Nah, it's my fault."

"No."

"I took the drugs." He laughed then. "The Verve were wrong. They did work."

"It doesn't matter, honey. There's no justice."

"There will be if I get rid of him."

"What do you mean?"

Outside, the roar of the helicopter filled the world, and a shadow crossed over the doorway. There were boots on the bottom steps. Gunfire.

"I'm tied to him. It's my fault. If I end it, I think I can end it all… and maybe find out what comes next. Pauline?"

"Yes, sweetie?"

"Find my mam and dad. Tell them I love them."

"I will, my love. I will."

"Right, well, it's been a pleasure. I wish I'd met you when I was alive. You're fucking awesome!"

Rob gripped his body by the back of the neck and closed his eyes for a moment. Then he stepped forward.

With tears in her eyes, Pauline watched the body of the dead rock star fall onto the conveyor and vanish in the dark. Behind her, the sound of heavy boots pounded on the stairs. She turned and raised a sad smile to the handsome soldier who burst through the door.

He raised his rifle and shot her between the eyes.

Glycerine

Rob couldn't move. He couldn't react. Pauline's body fell onto the conveyor, illuminated by the soldier's powerful torch before he calmly stepped back outside. It happened in an instant, but the belt had already taken Rob far away, the bright light of the open door a quickly receding rectangle shrinking in the distance. His body struggled beneath his ethereal feet, but he didn't care. The sadness was too much, and he turned to face his fate, utterly defeated. Ahead, the air shimmered where the conveyor dropped into hell.

This was it.

The end.

My zombie friend, the end.

Rob was scared. Terrified even. And he felt it as strongly as any pain he experienced when he was alive. He was convinced more than ever that this was hell, that he must have done something to deserve it. Perhaps it was the deaths of the young kids early in the night? Perhaps that was a test? Inaction was just the same as action when it came to questions of right and wrong, right? But it was a lesson he had learned too late. And the worst part, the absolute cherry on top of his steaming pile of sorrow and torment, was the fact he let Pauline die.

Well, at least it would be over soon. At least when his body dropped over the edge and vanished in the fire, he would finally, blessedly, wink out of existence into whatever came next. Truth be told, he hoped it was nothing.

Rob stood on his body as the conveyor moved, surfing his corpse towards the drop. He could hear the roar now, the thunder of the inferno. It sounded like a crowd. He lifted his arms wide, and closed his eyes, embracing it. Thoughts of Gavin Rossendale standing alone on a stage at Woodstock in front of thousands filled his mind. That was the dream. Just him and a guitar. Just him and the music. Singing his heart out while the world sang back. Was it too much to ask?

Maybe next time.

If there was a next time.

Rob closed his eyes and sang. It echoed in the metal tunnel, rising over the thunder of the conveyor and the fire. Damn, his voice sounded good in here. He'd really had a chance. He really could've been somebody.

It was too late now, though. He couldn't change it if he wanted to. Rob tried not to cry. He was so close. Nearly at the top. Smoke and the gathering steam filled the world as he drew closer. The air shimmered. The roar grew louder. It was like the moment before he walked on stage on *Stars in Their Eyes—was it really only a week ago*? Well, at least he did it, right? He fucking rocked the joint! Better to burn out than fade away. He closed his eyes as the pit opened.

The conveyor fell, and they tumbled, body and soul, in a shower of coke and ash. Deep, deep down into the inferno, into the depths of the great fire, and, just for a moment, just for a split second as the white-hot fire took him, Rob thought his body lifted a clenched fist with a raised thumb.

Rock and roll.

Loaded

That should have been the end.

Blinding lights, the final curtain, exit stage left. Thank you, San Dimas High! Goodnight!

But it wasn't.

It took Rob about twenty minutes of standing around inside the white-hot roaring inferno to realise he was not, finally, moving on to *whatever came next*.

This was it. This was the next. One night in Redcar with the dead.

But the zombies were gone.

His body was gone.

And he remained.

Sort of.

Rob lifted his hands to his face and saw… nothing.

"Interesting," he said. "That's going to make playing guitar a bit tricky."

In the end, Rob got bored of standing around waiting for the afterlife to present itself, so he walked out of the fire to find it.

Well, it *felt* like walking, but he didn't have any legs.

He drifted through the blast furnace, floated past the soldiers, and then flew over the golf course, though not before finding a certain young infantryman and causing his gun to malfunction. It was remarkably easy.

Rob was no longer encumbered by the memory of physical form, or even, he realised, any sense of obligation or morality. He simply didn't care.

All the doors were open. Every stage was his. He had a permanent backstage pass and keys to the city. Rob laughed as he flew away.

He was free to do what he wanted to do.

He was going to have a good time.

He was going to party.[22]

---

[22] A grim ending where the hero dies or turns into a poltergeist doesn't go down well with everyone, especially not certain mams who love happy endings and have never seen *Night of the Living Dead*, so this is just for them. This is the *real* ending. The burly soldier—who bears more than a passing resemblance to Jerome Flynn—rescues Pauline and carries her down the stairs like that scene in *An Officer and a Gentleman* (if you want, Pauline can do the carrying). He wraps her up nice and warm and fetches a cup of tea. By the time he comes back, Pauline has fixed up her hair and looks fucking fabulous, and the Alsatian from the car yard is by her side. The soldier loves dogs. So does Pauline. They all move in together, and Rob visits on a Sunday after haunting the Yorkshire Puddings at his mam and dad's house.

There. The End. Maybe.

Acknowledgements

A huge thank you to every person who beta-read the early drafts of this novel and the *many* iterations it went through before arriving here. Your input was invaluable (especially with regards to copyright laws!) Man, I hope I don't forget anyone… Ross, Mark, Matt, Zane, Monty (*you terrible ****!*), Louise, Si, Hogzy, Sam, Erica, Greg, April, Nikki, Mike, Brianna, Brendan, Megan, and of course, Kel, who doesn't like scary stuff but read it anyway.

What an absolute journey this silly, gross, bad-taste, little love letter to the '90s has had. You really put up with some nonsense, didn't you :-D

And finally, a massive thank you to Laura of @Hello_Moon_Creative for the front cover art. Laura is a tattoo artist from Redcar and a freaking genius! You should definitely check out her work.

Milton Keynes UK
Ingram Content Group UK Ltd.
UKHW020231241024
450133UK00007B/539

9 798227 573490